A CONSPIRACY OF TALKERS

A Conspiracy of Talkers

BY

Gaetano Savatteri

Translated from the Italian
By Steve Eaton

Italica Press
New York & Bristol
2021

Italian Original: *La congiura dei loquaci*
Copyright © 2000 Sellerio Editore

Translation Copyright © 2020 Steve Eaton

Italica Press Italian Crime Writers Series

ITALICA PRESS, INC.
99 Wall Street, Suite 650
New York, New York 10005

Library of Congress Cataloging-in-Publication Data
Names: Savatteri, Gaetano, 1964- author. | Eaton, Steve, 1959- translator.
Title: A conspiracy of talkers / by Gaetano Savatteri ; translated from the
  Italian by Steve Eaton.
Other titles: Congiura dei loquaci. English
Description: New York : Italica Press, 2021. | Series: Italian crime
  writers series | Summary: "Using the genre of crime fiction, Savatteri
  investigates various institutions of Italian culture - the community,
  the police, the justice system, the church, the family, the
  intelligentsia, and even the mafia- to explore and explain serious
  systemic problems of recent Italian history"-- Provided by publisher.
Identifiers: LCCN 2020056254 (print) | LCCN 2020056255 (ebook) | ISBN
  9781599102436 (hardcover) | ISBN 9781599102443 (trade paperback) |
  ISBN 9781599102450 (kindle edition)
Classification: LCC PQ4879.A867 C6613 2021 (print) | LCC PQ4879.A867
  (ebook) | DDC 853/.914--dc23
LC record available at https://lccn.loc.gov/2020056254
LC ebook record available at https://lccn.loc.gov/2020056255

Cover Image: Pollina, Sicily, 20 October 1943. American soldiers and their
vehicles moving past residents along in a narrow street after the town fell to the
Allies. War Pool Photos from ACME. Photographer: Michael J. Ackerman.

For a Complete List of
Modern Italian Fiction
Visit our Web Site at
http://www.italicapress.com/index011.html

CONTENTS

〜

About the Author

Gaetano Savatteri (1964, Milan) grew up in Racalmuto, Sicily. In 1980 he co-founded the cultural journal *Malgrado Tutto* (In Spite of Everything, https://www.malgradotuttoweb.it/), of which he is still an editor and a contributor. He was a reporter for the newspapers *Giornale di Sicilia* and *L'indipendente* before working as a journalist on Italy's Canale 5 and Rete 4 TV networks. He is the author of several books on mafia culture and history, as well as an array of short stories and novels, and he has written for stage and screen. *A Conspiracy of Talkers (La congiura dei loquaci)* was his first novel and is his first work to appear in English. Today he lives and works in Rome.

About the Translator

Steve Eaton is an independent scholar and translator who lives with his wife Hu Hsueh-Tzu in Austin, Texas. His translations of short stories by Luigi Pirandello have appeared in the journals *Metamorphoses, The Journal of Italian Translation,* and *The Journal of the Pirandello Society of America.* His blog, *The Garden of Eaton,* can be read at https://gardenofeaton.home.blog/.

Introduction[1]

Place: A small town in the mountains of Sicily.

Time: November 1944, sixteen months after the bloody Anglo-American invasion that drove the German and Italian armies off the island, fourteen months after the Italian government, having deposed Benito Mussolini in a palace coup, announced it was switching sides and joining the Allies, even while half of its nation was still occupied by German forces. The war is over in Sicily, but six gruesome months of fighting still lie ahead on the peninsula.

A young Italian-American Marine lieutenant, serving in Naples with the OSS (Office of Strategic Services, a recently-formed branch of the U.S. military devoted to intelligence operations, the precursor to the CIA), is sent by a bigoted superior to the Sicilian town on a bullshit assignment: the recovery of eight stolen army trucks. But as he makes his way to the town on a terrifying jeep ride over half-destroyed mountain roads, the man he needs to interrogate, the town's mayor, is assassinated in the middle of the crowded main square.

War-torn Sicily is still nominally under the control of AMGOT, the Allied government of military occupation. Under the not-so-watchful eye of the occupiers, the remnants of Fascism vie with communists, labor unions, Sicilian separatists, the church, and a resurgent mafia for land, money, and power. Brigands roam the countryside, robbing and settling scores. These conflicts overlay the

1. This novel was published under the title *La congiura dei loquaci* (literally, the conspiracy of the talkative) in 2000 by Sellerio, and reissued in 2017.

seemingly permanent plagues of Sicilian life: the crushing, institutionalized poverty of its farmers, miners, and fishermen; the violent, exploitative power of the mafia; and the oppressive treatment of the island by the government in Rome. The journalist, novelist, and short-story writer Gaetano Savatteri could hardly have chosen a setting more pregnant with dramatic possibility.

And what a story he tells. A story of murder, poison pen letters, carefully crafted perjury, armed hijacking, incestual sex abuse, and hungry protesters gunned down by army troops, among other things. But as dramatic as the elements of Savatteri's reconstruction are, none of them feels contrived or false.

To cite a few examples...

...The massacre of demonstrators by Italian government troops (who should have been fighting the Nazis), discussed with smug approval by the town's gentlemen of leisure. Twenty-four demonstrators (including women and children) were killed and over one hundred and fifty were injured by the king's troops, using guns and hand grenades, on the streets of Palermo on October 19, 1944, in an incident that became known as *"la strage del pane"* — the bread massacre.[2]

...Large-scale theft in Italy of U.S. Army materiel. The military historian Rick Atkinson documents its industrial scale, quoting the American general in charge of supplies in Naples, who stated that "as much as one ship out of every five [from the U.S. to the Mediterranean theater] is stolen or wasted," and Atkinson goes on to cite several examples, including "an entire trainload of sugar [in Italy that] vanished, along with the train itself."[3]

2. See for example https://archive.is/20141125173414/http://www.famigliacristiana.it/articolo/strage-del-pane.aspx, accessed 9/6/2020

3. Rick Atkinson, *The Day of Battle: The War in Sicily and Italy, 1943–1944* (New York: Henry Holt, 2007), iBook edition, chapter 10,

...Italian-American GIs recruited by the OSS for intelligence operations in Italy. There were more than a few, including Biagio Max Corvo, who ran an entire operation behind enemy lines,[4] and the professional wrestler Joseph "Jumping Joe" Savoldi, who helped to smuggle an important scientist from behind Fascist lines and went undercover in Allied-occupied Naples to smash black market operations.[5]

...Sexual abuse of girls by their fathers. Surely this sometimes happens in all parts of the world, but the novelist Dacia Maraini, in her memoir of growing up in the Sicilian town of Bagheria after the war, makes it sound like a local institution: "The abuse was criticized but no one would dare to intervene in the authority of the father over his daughter which is ancient and, of all customs, one of the hardest to stamp out, even today." And she goes on to cite two horrifying examples in her hometown, "cases of public knowledge that everyone was aware of and would never be reported."[6]

"Four Horsemen." Elsewhere Atkinson makes it clear that the stolen goods did not go towards feeding a hungry population; a handful of black marketeers got wealthy selling staples at highly inflated prices while thousands starved.

4. Wolfgang Saxon, "Biagio M. Corvo, 74, Intelligence Officer During World War II," *New York Times*, June 7 1994, Section B page 7, https://www.nytimes.com/1994/06/07/obituaries/biagio-m-corvo-74-intelligence-officer-during-world-war-ii.html accessed 09/10/2020. My thanks to the author for telling me about Corvo.

5. Mike Sielski, "Star in the Shadows," *The Philadelphia Inquirer,* 9/11/2019, https://www.inquirer.com/sports/a/notre-dame-football-wwe-oss-penn-quakers-joe-savoldi-20190911.html accessed 09/10/2020.

6. Dacia Maraini, *Bagheria,* Scrittori Contemporanei Series (Milan: Rizzoli, 2007), p. 144. Translation my own. Elsewhere in her memoir, Maraini reveals that during her childhood she was sexually assaulted by an adult male relative (who suffered no repercussions), and earlier, by a U.S. Marine on the transport ship taking her family back to Italy from Japan after the war. Among many other literary productions, Maraini has herself made two important contributions to the *impegnato* crime-fiction genre, the novels *Isolina* (1985) and *Voci* (1994).

But an accurate, unblinking portrayal of a time, place and culture does not, by itself, make a great story. What makes this novel a pleasure to read is its people. The judge, who believes he is a paragon of integrity, but is too afraid for his own skin to play the part. The sister and the mistress of the murder victim, fighting each other for the coveted spot next to the mayor's casket during the visitation. The easygoing Father Gioacchino, who helps to finance his order by running a card game in the storeroom of its monastery. The alcoholic veteran of the First World War, suffering from what we would now call PTSD after being left for dead under a snowdrift on the Piave front. The parade of "witnesses" whose laboriously formal statements belie a cover-up. There are some thirty named characters of some importance in this short novel, all adroitly rendered with humor, empathy, and an absence of sentimentality. They include the lone American, Lieutenant Benjamin Adano, through whose eyes we see much of the story unfold. Adano, who has learned literary Italian by painstakingly sounding out Dante's poetry, meets his opposite in Nanà, who is trying to learn English by reading *Macbeth* aloud.

As entertaining and engaging as the characters are, they serve a deeper purpose: through them Savatteri investigates the essential institutions of Italian culture: the community, the police, the justice system, the church, the family, the intelligentsia, and even the mafia, judging it by the standard of its own creation myth as a cult of "men of honor," who defend the weak against the powerful. Nor does the American occupational government, represented by the young lieutenant, escape scrutiny. Each of these is tested in the context of a man being railroaded to prison for a crime he probably didn't commit. Will justice be served, or subverted?

Savatteri's ambitions for this story go well beyond the standard *giallo* and its core subspecies, the murder mystery.[7]

7.   The word *giallo* literally means "yellow" and has been used in Italy to refer to crime fiction in general since the 1920s, when the Milan

He continues the tradition of socially "committed" *(impegnato)* Italian writers who use the genre of crime fiction to shine a light on the serious systemic problems of their society, following in the footsteps of post-war authors such as Giorgio Scerbanenco, Loriano Macchiavelli, Andrea Camilleri (who supplied the warm afterward to this novel), and Leonardo Sciascia. He is also not the first to use the crime-fiction genre to explore and explain dark events in recent Italian history that have remained a "mystery" for all the wrong reasons. The deadly Piazza Fontana terrorist bombing in Milan in 1969 and the massive *Tangentopoli* ("Bribesville") corruption scandal of the 1990s are two examples of well-known events that became grist for *giallo* writers.[8] This story too is based on real events.

Those events are briefly described by the renowned Sicilian journalist, activist, and crime-fiction author Leonardo Sciascia (1921–89) in his memoir *Le parrocchie di Regalpetra* (The parishes of Regalpetra) (Bari: Laterza, 1956). In a few brushstrokes, Sciascia outlines the bare facts of the case: in November 1944, the mayor of Racalmuto, Sicily, an angry and litigious sort, is shot in the back of the neck as he strolls in the middle of the town's crowded main piazza on a Sunday evening. The killer somehow flees unhindered, but the police and public opinion instantly

publishing house Mondadori introduced a line of volumes in the genre with yellow covers. Although there's no universally accepted definition of what is or is not *giallo* literature, it's fair to take that genre as a starting point here, especially since this novel introduces an unsolved murder in the first sentence and makes more than a nodding reference to the life and crime-fiction novels of Leonardo Sciascia.

8.   See: Barbara Pezzotti, *Politics and Society in Italian Crime Fiction: An Historical Overview* (Jefferson, NC: McFarland, 2014). Among other works, Pezzotti mentions Diego Zandel's *Massacro per un Presidente* (Milan: Mondadori, 1981) (Massacre for a president), in relation to the Fontana bombing (p. 128) and lists five authors for whom "the devastating effects of Tangentopoli...are at the core..." of their works. (p. 134)

converge in suspecting one and only one perpetrator: a poor unemployed laborer with a criminal record who had been heatedly arguing with the mayor earlier in the day. The mayor was also a partner in the local sulfur mine, making him not only the town's dispenser of public aid and public works jobs but also its biggest private employer. The laborer is quickly convicted and sent to prison.

But Sciascia himself doesn't buy it. He believes the man might well have been capable of robbery, but not murder. And he should know. Sciascia grew up in Racalmuto, and, as he says, he knew the man.[9]

Savatteri also grew up in Racalmuto, though he was born in 1964, two decades after the mayor's murder. He uses his experience and background as a journalist and Sicilian, and his imagination as a novelist, to re-examine this story of crime and misdirected punishment. And unlike the infamous Fontana bombing and the *Tangentopoli* affair, the sordid events that form the core of this novel would likely have languished in obscurity if Savatteri had not brought them into the light with all of their uncomfortable truths.

There is a proverb Savatteri uses to describe an incompetent defense attorney's philosophy towards serving his clients: *"la miglior parola e' quella che non si dice,"* or loosely "silence is the best defense." In this era of misinformation, disinformation, and "alternative facts," this author reminds us that speaking up and telling the whole story is more important than ever.

Steve Eaton
Austin, September 2020

---

9.   Leonardo Sciascia, *Le parrocchie di Regalpetra* (Milan: Adelphi, 1991) 2016, iBook edition, "Sindaci e commissari," locs. 897–913

List of Characters

ADANO, BENJAMIN: U.S. Marine Corps lieutenant currently attached to the OSS (Office of Strategic Services) headquarters in Naples; a New Yorker of Italian heritage who is fluent in formal Italian. In civilian life, he is a scholar of Italian literature. He is under orders to investigate the hijacking of American army trucks near a town in Sicily.

ASARO, TOTÒ: Lackey and hit-man for PAPANDRÈ, also coached by Papandrè as witness against PICIPÒ.

BAMMINO, TANO, see DI LORO, CICCIO ALAIMO.

BARBARO: SARETTA TAIBBI's lover.

BARTOLOTTA, GERLANDO CIOTTA: Hitman working for CALÒ VIZZINI.

BRUCCULERI, PROFESSOR: A regular of the town's *casino* or social club.

CARACCO, SEBASTIANO: Traumatized, alcoholic veteran of World War One (the "Great War"), who can provide an alibi for PICIPÒ.

CASTIGLIONE, BLASCO DI: Hero of the historical novel *I Beati Paoli* by the Sicilian writer Luigi Natoli (1857-1941) and a figure in CICCIO ALAIMO DI LORO's puppet show.

DI DIO: Police sergeant serving under PEREZ.

DI LORO, CICCIO ALAIMO: Travelling storyteller who works with puppeteer Tano Bammino. Their tales of righteous revenge strike a chord with ANGELO PICIPÒ, Vincenzo's son.

Collura, Enrico: Farrauto's bodyguard; violently slaps Vincenzo Picipò for acting aggressively towards the mayor shortly before the latter is killed.

Falletta, Mommino: Lackey for Papandrè; coached by Papandrè as witness against Picipò.

Farrauto, Adelina: Sister and dependent of Baldassare Farrauto.

Farrauto, Baldassare: Murder victim; mayor of the town, appointed by the American army; operator of a local sulfur mine and dispenser of public jobs and aid.

Gesafatti, Graziella: A young woman who claims to have witnessed Picipò's wife Maria frantically searching for her husband at the time of the murder; she is the lover of Nicolò.

Giangreco: A lawyer and a regular of the town's *casino* or social club.

Giglio, Rosina: Cousin of Papandrè, who uses her as a plant to lead police to Graziella Gesafatti, whose testimony will help convict Picipò.

Gioacchino, Father: Priest who runs a card game in the warehouse of his monastery to raise money for his order. He seems to know about the stolen trucks.

Hundred-Ten: See Picipò, Vincenzo.

Judge: Retired attorney who presides over the local court.

Maranella, Andrea Restivo: Also known as Papandrè, a local mafia boss.

Merulla, Maria: Wife of Vincenzo Picipò.

Mulè, Ignazio: A regular of the town's *casino* or social club.

Nanà (Young man in the club): A member of the social club who works for the local farm co-op. Some readers recognize in this character the future journalist, activist and writer of crime fiction Leonardo Sciascia (1921–89), a native son of Racalmuto, Sicily.

NANÌA: Corporal in the police under PEREZ; he is ill after returning from several days of leave, spent drinking and eating in his hometown.

NICOLÒ: A young man coached by PAPANDRÈ as a witness who saw MARIA MERULLA anxiously searching for her husband at the time of the murder. Lover of GRAZIELLA GESAFATTI, who will support his story.

PAPANDRÈ, see MARANELLA, ANDREA RESTIVO.

PEREZ: Chief of the local carabinieri (police). Holds the rank of *maresciallo,* a non-commissioned officer.

PICIPÒ, ANGELO: Eldest son of VINCENZO PICIPÒ and MARIA MERULLA.

PICIPÒ, SALVATORE: Middle son of VINCENZO PICIPÒ and MARIA MERULLA.

PICIPÒ, PINO: Youngest son of VINCENZO PICIPÒ and MARIA MERULLA.

PICIPÒ, VINCENZO: Also known as Hundred-Ten; an unemployed mineworker, prime suspect in BALDASSARE FARRAUTO's murder. He is married to MARIA MERULLA and is the father of Angelo, Salvatore, and Pino.

SACCOMANDA, LUCINA: The longtime mistress of the late mayor and the unknowing heiress of his property.

SEMINO: BENJAMIN ADANO's driver, local guide and interpreter. Born in the United States but raised in his father's hometown in Sicily.

SPOTO PULEO, ANGELO: Town clerk. He customarily accompanies the mayor on his nightly walk home from the piazza; he witnesses the shooting.

Taibbi, Gabriele: Petty criminal, sexual predator of his daughter, Saretta Taibbi. Papandrè's thugs ask him to hide a pistol that will be used to kill the mayor, Baldassare Farrauto. His daughter's anonymous letter falsely accuses him of intending to kill Farrauto.

Taibbi, Saretta: Daughter and victim of Gabriele Taibbi, and Barbaro's lover. She sends a letter, falsely accusing her father of planning to kill Baldassare Farrauto, to Lucina Saccomanda.

Vizzini, Calò: Regional mafia capo, Papandrè's superior, business partner of Baldassare Farrauto, and a historical figure.

A Conspiracy of Talkers

I knew the man, I wouldn't have doubted his guilt for some theft. I would never have believed him capable of murder. But anyone can make a mistake — me, the judges, I daresay even a chief of the carabinieri can make a mistake.

Le parrocchie di Regalpetra, Leonardo Sciascia

Mr. Benjamin Adano
622 Oaks Ridge Road
Franklin Lakes
New Jersey
USA

Signor Lieutenant Adano,

you must excuse me that I didn't write sooner but I just got back home and now I found your address still good I hope.

Pardon my writing that I learned in prison, I want to say thanks for the help you gave my family in my absence. I don't know if you found out they don't live in the town any more I couldn't find anyone. But I hope to rejoin my sons soon.

It was many years ago my troubles started maybe you still remember on November 6 1944...

NIGHT

1

The mayor died shortly before 9 p.m. Killed by a small-caliber projectile, he was a blotch in the miserly light leaking out of the Cacioppo Café. Sprawling face down, his light-colored raincoat spattered with blood, his arms still outstretched as if to break his last fall. An empty circle in the crowd marked his presence in the middle of the narrow piazza.

Ten men, trapped in the café, had retreated to the rear of the premises. Corporal Nanìa, cold and tired, was taking down their names. He was aware that none of them would make any contribution to the useless investigation that — Nanìa was certain — would nonetheless drag on all night. A wasted, interminable night for Nanìa, who'd returned just that morning from four days' leave for Day of the Dead festivities, his belly still swollen with fig cake and marzipan treats and strong homemade wine.

The judge was forcing his way through the current of astonishment and fear spreading out from the mayor's corpse. They had tracked down the judge at his mother-in-law's place. When the carabinieri knocked, a peppercorn from the cheese a shepherd delivered to the house once a week went down the wrong way. Town judge for three years, he'd been getting a steady paycheck after finally shuttering his attorney's practice. He couldn't take it anymore, having to defend perpetrators of livestock rustling and crop theft. He had restored his own personal sense of justice, a torch he claimed to hold high and bright. But he hadn't gotten used to that pounding on the door, which still made him jump every time. And there was another reason for his sudden agitation, for the questioning look he exchanged with his equally startled wife: he needed a moment — a rather long moment — to convince himself that the carabinieri at the door didn't represent a threat, even for a judge. Especially for a judge.

Pale, shocked, he examined the corpse. He flinched, seeing the rivulet of blood seeping out from under its head.

The mayor was a bully. There wasn't a soul in town with whom he hadn't had some dispute. And he had enough lawsuits going in all the courts in the province to keep at least seven lawyers in his pay.

The judge studied the victim again. He'd appeared before his court more than once, always as the plaintiff, with his arrogant, disdainful expression. He had faith in the written law because he had at his disposal a force that did not appear in any government acts, in any official documents or binders. The judge had noticed the weight of that force even in his own courtroom, of which he was the master and final authority. He sensed that the uniformed officers standing behind him meant nothing. The presence that accompanied the mayor as he entered the courtroom changed the way even they walked and talked.

He breathed a sigh of relief, that judge. Then he looked around, afraid that someone might have noticed. But all eyes were fixed on the corpse.

The mayor was dead, murdered. And the judge believed that all the others too, all those standing around the body with blank expressions, were privately rejoicing. Sulfur miners, salt miners, peasants, day laborers, reapers, vine tenders, carpenters, cart drivers: every one of them had a good reason for feeling no grief over the mayor's death, for actually feeling relief and elation.

The man had always been a bully, but even more so, to the point of blindness, as soon as the Americans appointed him mayor right after the landing. They'd arrived in July of the previous year, quickly occupying the town without encountering the least resistance. Even the homes of diehard Fascists flew the stars and stripes, sewn by prudent hands in the shadow and uncertainty of the eve of the invasion.

Operator of a sulfur mine, he had friends and allies everywhere. Before the war, those same friends had gotten him thrown in jail, identifying him as a mafia capo. But he was released with an acquittal — bad news for anyone who'd denounced him.

The judge looked for the dark uniform of Chief Perez, head of the local carabinieri. He was near the entrance of the Cacioppo Café, the buttons of his jacket pulled down over his fat belly. The town considered the chief an idiot. But he was a certain kind of idiot, good at understanding men and things, good enough to make you believe that idiots are equipped with a sort of compass that keeps them out of the worst trouble, faithfully pointing out the right direction.

The chief greeted the judge with cordial irritation. He in turn considered the judge inept, even dangerous, unreliable because fixated on a search for some abstract ideal of honesty.

"Your Honor, who could have imagined?" said the chief.

The judge shook his head. Anyone could have imagined. Many were *hoping*. If there was anyone who might end up murdered, it was precisely the mayor.

Nanìa joined in. "Nothing. These guys are saying they didn't see anything. They just heard a shot, but it sounded like a firecracker."

The chief shrugged, turning to the judge. Since the Allied landing less than a year and a half before, there'd been at least three homicides per month. Deserters killed in the countryside, miners with their throats cut along a mule path. They'd shot a carpenter in front of the cathedral, but that was a matter of jealousy. No one ever saw anything, no one ever knew. The chief, who perhaps wasn't such a profound idiot, would manage to find out something — the husband of the lover of the carpenter ended up under arrest — but always via indirect paths and informants, vaguely identified in the record as "voices of public opinion."

"Your Honor, I have to go to the station," the chief said to the judge. "If you want to go home after concluding the formalities with Corporal Nanìa, don't worry. We'll handle things. It's damp out tonight."

The judge was stunned by this maternal solicitude. If anything, Chief Perez had always harbored a bit of envy for the judge, for the home where his wife had by now filled a bedwarmer with hot coals and placed it under the sheets.

"Damp, yes. Nice weather for the dead." The judge barely uttered the phrase before realizing how inappropriate it was. But he'd only meant the festival, with its sweets made of dried figs and almonds that heralded the coming winter.

"Don't worry, Your Honor, we've already notified the family. Go get some rest. We'll be here."

"He's hot on the trail," thought the judge, who loved the tales and terminology of the hunt, even if he himself had not taken aim at a rabbit recently. Appearing in the countryside carrying a rifle had lately become too perfect an opportunity for anyone who wanted to get rid of you, shedding tears afterwards over the unfortunate accident.

Chief Perez left in a hurry, crossing the piazza. His ample shadow sliced through the yellow light from the shops still open. In front of the cathedral, he stopped to speak to two men. All three disappeared around the corner, heading towards the police station.

"The righteous one pays for the sinner," thought the judge. The phrase suddenly erupted from childhood memories. Those words bore the rhythm and tone of his mother when she spoke them, of helpless resignation and complacent suffering.

The judge turned back to the mayor's corpse. He was struck by the terrifying idea that here before him was an act of justice, substantial and concrete. Unlike his judgments.

"Shall we conclude the formalities, Your Honor?" the voice of Nanìa roused him.

"Let's conclude, Corporal, let's conclude."

2

"I can't even think about it, Signor Lieutenant. If we hadn't been *laki, veri laki*, we'd be with the souls in purgatory right now."

The jeep was lurching down the road. Its headlights revealed gaps in the pavement, avoided at the last second with a sudden skid. Lieutenant Adano's knuckles were white from the effort of hanging onto the vehicle for hours. It was raining. The dust on the windshield had turned into a dark coating of mud.

"Are you sure you can see all right?" the lieutenant asked Semino in Italian.

"*Donworri*, Lieutenant. Eyes like a cat, Lieutenant."

Once more Lieutenant Adano leafed through his mental phrasebooks — from the Italian dialect of his grandfather to the Sicilian-American of his aunt Cettina, whom he'd listened to as a child. He came back to Semino's words, still not trusting in the road. Or the driver.

Sure, *veri laki*. E*xtremely laki* along a hairpin curve on the mountain road near Vicari, where the jeep had careened sideways on two wheels helplessly skidding, unable to gain traction, spewing rocks and dust. From his side, Adano saw almond trees flying towards him. Semino's face didn't change — he had the same silent, focused expression since leaving Palermo. He managed to bring the jeep to a stop, the back half dangling in midair. With the help of some peasants, they'd managed to get back on the road and on their way. But from that moment — he hadn't said a word before — Semino didn't stop talking.

He told Lieutenant Adano about his grandfather Calogero Castrenze who emigrated to New York before the Great War, about his years in Brooklyn and then his move to Buffalo, about the fact that he'd been the best shoemaker in his hometown, but there was hunger, not even *crustabred* to eat, and that's why he'd left with his wife and four children. Two had died but the girl, his mother, married someone from back home who lived in Buffalo and he, Salvatore, was born in America, but they'd always called him Sam though his mother used to call him Semino, bless her soul, which was surely in heaven, a sainted woman who'd made sacrifices so he and his brother could grow up healthy but she died when Semino was ten, *tenny ears*, so his father went back home to get married because a man with two kids can't stay single and even in America there was the Depression so it might've been better if his grandfather had emigrated to Americazuela or Argentina cause there you just had to find some piece of open land, build a house on it and say this is mine, *maicauntri*, but instead his father went back to the old country and married a woman who, with all due respect, Signor Lieutenant, was no good for my father, who'd returned from America and maybe forgot how things worked back home, so she had a son seven months after the wedding, they said he was born premature but even my father knew he was the son of a whore, *sonnovibich*, he got depressed and didn't want to go back to America with a son who, *realli*, wasn't his son so he stayed in Sicily but Semino and his brother Charlie, his real brother, were always called Americans and then when the war ended and you guys arrived which was *the save for la Sicilia*, knowing the language, he worked for the Americans in Palermo, so good that once even General Poletti asked for his help on a sensitive matter, a *serious thing* which he did so well that General Poletti, a true gentleman, told Semino that he was a real *american man*, it is a great honor to America and to

Sicily that we are like brothers, closer, even, *duiuandersten*, Lieutenant?"

Sure, of course. Adano understood less than half of the speech, that garble of Sicilianized English, of Sicilian in *swing americano*. But mostly what he understood was that he had misled Semino from the beginning, when he disclosed that he knew Italian. He'd studied at City College, painstakingly sounding out Dante, Petrarch, Boccaccio. Nights of reading and rereading, savoring the sonorous language, musical and full, "the gentle hue of oriental sapphire," so different and so distant from the Italian of his aunt Cettina, gloomy and muddled, mournful and drawling. Now that mournfulness, even more unhinged, was churning, churning in Semino's words, in this November evening, in the driving rain, in the road that twisted and turned, turning away even from the feeble lights of distant towns and plunging again into the blackness of the countryside, and in the shadows of the men on mules who fled to the side of the road at the sight of headlights.

"How much longer, Semino?"

"*Innotime*, Signor Lieutenant. Past that rock."

The rock spur rose before them, white in the dark, wet night. *"Chi passa dalla rocca e non è rubato, o il brigante dorme o è malato,"* Semino chanted. *If you get past the rock with no gun to your chest, then the bandit is sick or taking a rest.*

"There were bandits around here?"

"There still are, Lieutenant, but *donworri*, they don't do anything to the Americans. You're American, right?"

Semino had asked this question, formulated one way or another, three times now. He just couldn't believe that Lieutenant Adano was really the American officer whose arrival in Palermo from Naples he'd been informed of five days before, with orders to act as guide and interpreter. This guy here seemed to speak proper mainland Italian, even though he swore that his father and grandfather were Sicilian.

"Why don't they do anything to the Americans, Semino?"

"Respect, Signor Lieutenant. They respect the Americans, like we all do."

Beyond the rock, the dim lights of the town came into view — a few lit windows, a row of lights strung along the main road, bobbing in the wind.

Semino drove confidently — he knew the area. He'd been there the year before, when it was a zone of operations a few kilometers from the beaches of Licata and Gela and the confused and deadly landings that Adano had learned about later from accounts of veterans he'd met in Naples.

At the time, Adano was in the Pacific, relegated to a base without name or importance, shuffling papers and stamping documents. A Top Priority mission, they'd told him, just as his emergency transfer to Naples four months ago was Top Priority, pulling him out of the Marines and attaching him to the OSS. A promotion: now the papers he shuffled and the documents he stamped were marked "SECRET." Top Priority, that's also what Major Stafford said as he handed Adano the bundle of documents for his mission in Sicily. His orders were to find out what had happened to eight trucks, originally consigned to the 2nd Armored Division of Patton's Seventh Army, then to AMGOT (the allied occupational government), and then disappearing, stolen or stripped for parts. Eight vanished trucks: Top Priority.

The jeep stopped in front of the Hotel Roma. Semino honked. The entrance behind the glass door lit up.

The man who came out of the *pensione* embraced Semino, kissing him on the cheeks. He was missing a hand — a stump stuck out of one sleeve. He stepped forward obsequiously. "*Prego*, Signor Lieutenant. I speak English."

"*Non si preoccupi, parlo italiano,*" Adano replied, and continued in Italian. "Is City Hall nearby? First thing tomorrow morning, I have to see the mayor."

The man's eyes opened wide. Surprised and maybe disappointed, thought Adano, by my perfect Italian.

"The mayor?" He tried to catch Semino's eyes. Then he turned back to Adano. "The mayor, you said?"

"The mayor, Signor Farrauto." Adano reached for his leather portfolio. He'd read and reread the documents. He was sure. Baldassare Farrauto, appointed in August 1943, was mayor of this town.

The proprietor of the hotel gasped, glancing around at the deserted street. He approached Semino and whispered something incomprehensible, a gesture more than a word.

Semino remained expressionless, with the same blank face he wore while half of the jeep was dangling in midair off a turn on the mountain road near Vicari.

"The mayor had an accident. Two hours ago. They shot him, *duiuandersten*, Signor Lieutenant? He's dead."

3

A light coughing fit.

Vincenzo Picipò didn't open his eyes, because he'd never closed them. In the damp, cold darkness he turned towards Pino, his youngest son, lying on his side. The child was asleep, the delicate outline of his face pressed into the pillow. No, he hadn't awakened.

Another coughing fit, more severe. Pino was sick. Over the summer, the cough seemed to dry up, but now with the dampness that formed crusts of salt on the plaster walls, with the rain turning the streets to mud, it returned worse than ever. The doctor said the little boy was weak, white as an angel, a bit anemic.

An angel. A plaster angel like the ones in the shrine of the Madonna.

Pino was still asleep, but his breathing had become labored. Vincenzo got up and turned to his son, touching his forehead: it was soaked. Maybe the boy was dreaming. At the touch of his hand, the child turned, a brief moan escaping his lips.

"Vincenzo, what is it?" His wife had awakened.

"Nothing. Pino's sleeping."

"So let him sleep." Whispers in the little room, the sounds of their breathing and those of their three sons.

"Is it raining?" asked Maria.

Vincenzo went to the door. "No, it's stopped."

"Come back to bed. It's cold."

Vincenzo Picipò stepped over his eldest son, sleeping on a wooden trunk by the door.

"Does it still hurt?"

"No, it's nothing."

"Vincenzo, you have to let it go, those people are arrogant."

"I know what I'm doing. You don't have to tell me."

"All right, fine, but don't shout or you'll wake up Pinuzzo."

They were in bed, the blankets feeling heavy and damp on top of them. Eyes open, looking up at the ceiling.

His wife stared at him. "Are you upset?"

"Why should I be upset?"

"You're not sleeping."

"So what? I don't have to go down to the mine tomorrow."

His wife didn't respond. She knew Vincenzo didn't have to go down to the mine. He hadn't worked for four months. She knew that when Vincenzo wasn't working, bad things happened. He was hotblooded, and when there was no money, his blood boiled until even at night she would feel him moving, squirming, grinding his teeth.

Vincenzo Picipò was an unlucky man. And his character didn't help. He was fourteen years old when, true to form, he stabbed a cart driver who wouldn't give him a ride. Luckily the carter survived, but from that day on the courts and the carabinieri never gave Vincenzo a moment of peace. Eventually they sent him to the prison farm in the Tremiti Islands — thirteen months away from home. His oldest boy, Angelo, was only two. And she, carrying the baby, would go to harvest wheat in the countryside outside of town, her eyes glued to the hazelnut trees where Angelo fell asleep, worn out by the heat. She was afraid the snakes would bite him, attracted by the lingering smell of her milk.

The streets were quiet. Until an hour ago they kept hearing hurried steps, urgent voices. There was trouble in the town, but Maria was unaware of it. She was too anxious to think about what was going on outside.

Vincenzo had come home with a swollen eye, his left cheek marked by a cut. Stinking of wine. Unwilling to explain, he only muttered some insult and then got into bed. The neighbors, women who were visiting Maria, rushed off, put out by the man's behavior. He was always ill-mannered, but this was really too much.

A night of bad things and wicked deeds. And Maria remained anxious until Angelo came home — he was fifteen now and thought he was a man and came home late every night. Only then had Maria shut the door, with relief.

"What time is it?" muttered Vincenzo.

"I can't tell from here."

Vincenzo got out of bed, cursing.

"Do you have to use such language?"

Picipò didn't answer. He was by the clock. "It's midnight."

Steps outside the door. A fist rapping on the door, then pounding. Pounding again.

"Picipò, open up. It's me, the chief."

Pino awoke, coughing. Maria sat up in bed.

Vincenzo opened the door. The cold rain-soaked air rushed into the room, wrenching the other two boys from their sleep.

"What's going on, Chief?"

In the dim light from the street, the chief's outline filled up the doorway. He shoved Vincenzo aside, a flash of metal in his fist.

"Let's have some light. Now."

Maria was trembling as she looked for the lamp. Her hands had forgotten how to strike a match.

The light revealed the boys' sleepy, stunned faces. Pino was coughing.

Vincenzo was standing by the clock in long woolen underwear and a yellowed army undershirt. He understood.

It wasn't the first time the night was torn open like this. It had happened before, it would happen again. Or maybe not.

Chief Perez, putting his gun back in its holster, pointed at the jacket, black pants, and dark beret sitting on the chair by the bed. "Those yours?"

Vincenzo Picipò looked at him in surprise. Those were all the clothes he had, good for summer and winter. Everyone he knew in town had one suit, black. It hides the stains.

"Let's go to the station."

Pino was crying and coughing.

Chief Perez turned to Sergeant Di Dio. "Sergeant, conduct the search. Though we're not going to find anything."

"What are you looking for, Chief?"

"You know, Picipò."

Vincenzo felt the blood pounding in his chest, in his temples, in his hands. "You're making a mistake, Chief. I was sleeping. You saw yourself."

"You were awake, Picipò, you opened the door before we finished knocking. Don't take me for an idiot. I've been around longer than you."

Vincenzo got dressed. Pino was in his mother's arms. Angelo, the eldest, put a hand on his brother Salvatore's shoulder. He watched his father's movements: he was pulling his pants on over his long woolen underwear.

The sergeant was sullenly opening the drawers of the credenza, a pure formality.

Maria stayed silent. They had taken him away before, but this time the grief made her eyes well up.

"Chief, can I kiss my sons?"

Maria had never seen Vincenzo kiss his sons. A slap sometimes, never a kiss. "What should we do, Vincenzo?" she sobbed.

Her husband didn't answer. He kissed Pino, then Salvatore, and when he got to Angelo, he put a hand on his shoulder. "You know..."

The boy nodded.

They went out, Vincenzo in front and the chief behind. The sergeant slowly continued his search, avoiding the boys' looks. It was raining again. A soft, light rain.

4

E quindi uscimmo a riveder le stelle. And so we emerged to see the stars once more. But there were no stars, or moon, in the sky. Benjamin Adano switched off the lamp and looked out the window. The sky didn't provide any light. A soft rain was falling, almost invisibly. The street was dark now, the blackout still in effect. But no aircraft, German or Allied, had crossed these skies in a year or more.

Lieutenant Adano turned on the lamp next to his bed, again. He was still in uniform. There wouldn't be any water in the hotel until morning, they'd told him. All he had was a jugful, enough to rinse his face.

Beneath his window, until a few minutes earlier, two men had stopped to have an urgent conversation, despite the rain. A light rain, barely perceptible — the peasants out in the fields would ignore it until they got soaking wet. There was a word in the local dialect for this kind of fitful rain, but it didn't come to Lieutenant Adano's mind. He couldn't quite retrieve it from the lost tongue of his aunt Cettina, the woman who'd raised him after his mother's death.

Even the two men dressed in black, as black as the night without light or stars, were muttering words in a dialect Adano couldn't quite make out. He'd remained silent, on the bed, documents scattered on the blanket, trying to snatch some phrase or word from the continuous guttural murmur. Useless.

He went back to reading the documents he'd brought from Naples. He lined them up on the bed once more. But he'd already committed them to memory.

The last reported theft of a truck by bandits who stopped the driver, brandishing firearms — "They respect the

Americans," so believed Semino — occurred in June. The other six reports bore earlier dates, starting in September 1943. The second truck was stolen in November '43, another before Christmas of the same year, then in January '44, in March, two in a single strike in May. And then the last one in June.

The Anglo-American forces had left Sicily in February 1944, but some garrisons remained, put in place by the Allied Military Government for Occupied Territories, which administered what little was left to administer.

The order to investigate had come directly from General Poletti's office. He considered those trucks his personal property, like everything else run by AMGOT, first in Sicily, then in Naples. The request had made the rounds of bureaus, commands, and agencies before inexplicably winding up on the desk of the OSS. And there it might have been forgotten, as happened to so many other documents in that war made up of deaths, papers, rubber stamps, and pointless dispatches.

If Poletti hadn't run into Major Stafford at a reception, if Major Stafford hadn't been sharply reprimanded in front of a Neapolitan lady who'd been granting him certain favors for the last two months, if Stafford hadn't considered Poletti a mafioso and all Italians criminals, if the next day he hadn't come across Lieutenant Adano on the steps of the palazzo on the Corso Umberto that housed the OSS headquarters, and considering the lieutenant an Italian like all the rest, hadn't decided to proceed with the investigation, entrusting it to the aforesaid Lieutenant Adano precisely to keep it a matter among Italians, ensuring that Poletti would be both properly obeyed and properly screwed (since the case of the vanishing trucks would go nowhere)...if all this hadn't happened in that precise yet random chain of events, Benjamin Adano would never have set foot in the Sicily of his grandfather Beniamino and aunt Cettina and wouldn't be here, now, in a dark and nearly silent town, where they'd just murdered the man who might have been able to give him some kind, *any* kind, of evasive answer that would have allowed him (with a note in the margin: "ANSWER: NEGATIVE") to quickly complete his mission.

But the mayor died shortly before 9 p.m., and Lieutenant Adano would never get to ask him if he knew or might suspect something, seeing as how the eight trucks had all vanished along the road from town to the Iacuzzo Pietrebianche Sulfur Mine. He'd never get to ask him how it could be that in recent months the town's cart drivers were complaining because their work had been cut back, even gathering before City Hall to throw rocks at the windows of the mayor's office. Yet down at Porto Empedocle, the business of shipping sulfur from the Iacuzzo Pietrebianche Mine was humming along like never before, thanks in part to a new transportation service equipped with a ragtag fleet of trucks.

And he'd never get to ask Mayor Baldassare Farrauto what he knew about all of this, even though he'd been the sole operator of the mine since March 1941 and mayor of the town from August 1943. They'd shot him while he was out for a walk in the middle of the piazza, accompanied by his usual bodyguard who this time hadn't guarded anybody, nor drawn the revolver he always kept in his pocket, nor pursued whoever had fired the small-caliber pistol round that, striking the occipital lobe from behind, had smashed the mayor's brain, instantly commending his soul to God or, presumably, to that eternal fire which almost all of his constituents wished for him.

De' violenti il primo cerchio è tutto, whispered Adano. *The first circle is filled with the violent.* But he couldn't go any further, nor could he manage to place the line in the eleventh or twelfth canto of the *Inferno*. He opened his suitcase and pulled out his pocket *Dante Hoepliano*, with notes and introductory remarks by Dr. Rafaello Fornaciari, 1920 edition, a present from his father when Benjamin was barely two years old. He always carried it with him, that miniature *Divina Commedia*. He'd often asked himself how much that one gift, supremely useless for a child of two, as useless as all the gestures and all the equally useless but more hurtful absences of his father, had weighed on his life, ultimately leading to a degree in Italian literature and Renaissance history. A degree of little use anywhere, especially on the streets of New York.

He stepped towards the window and opened the little book to the beginning.

> *Nel mezzo del cammin di nostra vita*
> *Mi ritrovai per una selva oscura*
> *Ché la diritta via era smarrita*
> *Ah quanto a dir qual era, è cosa dura...*

Halfway along the road of life, I found myself in a dark forest, having lost the true path. Ah, it's a hard thing to describe, what that was... "Lieutenant!"

Adano roused himself, realizing he'd been reciting the verses out loud.

"Lieutenant, *haviuneed* of me?" Semino whispered from behind the door.

"What?"

"Do you need something, Lieutenant, are you okay? Did you call?"

"No, don't worry."

"So I can go ahead and sleep?"

"Yes, I don't need anything."

"*Goodnait*, then."

"Good night, Semino."

Adano set the *Divina Commedia* on the nightstand. He switched off the lamp, he tried to sleep, he got into bed still in uniform — the room was cold. But he couldn't manage to drift off. He was too exhausted.

He remembered that his duffel bag held a manual stolen from a British colonel, a guidebook for officers involved in the landing of Montgomery's Eighth Army in Sicily. It bore the designation SECRET but was as dull and bland as a tourist guide for Englishmen on vacation. Maybe good for getting sleepy. He opened it at random to chapter five, CHARACTERISTICS OF THE PEOPLE.

> *The population may be divided into the rich nobility, the poor nobility, the rich middle class, the middle class and the people. The noisy superficial nature of the Neapolitans is not characteristic of the Sicilians, to whom it is very unsympathetic. Bolton King declares in his History of United Italy: "In contrast to the gay and shallow Neapolitan, the Sicilian is silent, laconic and brave..."*

The manual slipped out of his hands, his eyes closing, as Benjamin Adano thought confusedly about history, clichés, boredom, the national character of a people, about Sicilians and Americans and the English, but not long enough to draw a common thread. Sleep was rapidly untying his thoughts. Outside, the rain had just stopped.

5

"You were walking down the street?"

"I was going along with my head down, like I was minding my own business."

"And..."

"The chief called my name, twice."

"And..."

"How was I supposed to know anything? I was on my way home."

"And this is good. Get it, Mommino?"

Mommino Falletta took a deep drag on his cigarette. There were already three stubs under his heel. He only nodded with his eyes.

"You were evasive..."

"What?"

"Evasive, evasive. You didn't really know what happened..."

"I knew exactly, Papandrè, but I was holding back."

"And this is good...get it, Mommino?"

Not speaking, Mommino snuffed out one more cigarette with his heel.

"Why can't you act civilized, Mommino?" gasped Papandrè, pointing to the ashes on the floor, wheezing.

Mommino bent down.

"Leave it, leave it. Pay attention, pay attention."

Mommino dropped the butts back on the floor.

Papandrè snorted angrily. He turned back to Totò Asaro and placed a hand on his knee. Affectionately.

"They took you to the station?"

"Immediately. I waited in a chair outside the chief's office. Then Enrico Collura came out, and they made me go in."

"Did Enrico tell you anything?"

"Nothing. I said hello. Like usual."

Papandrè's white shirt stretched over his belly. His chest rose and fell in asthmatic spasms. "You told them what you knew."

"But all I knew was I had come here to say what happened in the piazza..."

"Did they ask you why you came here?"

"Everyone knows you're related to the mayor, and you're his friend, almost like a brother."

"That's what the chief said?"

"No, but when *I* said so he just shook his head. So did the sergeant."

"But it's a fact...right?"

Mommino was distracted, entranced by the painting of the Madonna of the Mountain, which the lightbulb barely revealed. And also entranced by the infernal demons squirming at the Madonna's feet, trying to see if he recognized any faces.

"Mommino, are you asleep?"

"Please, Papandrè, I'm right here," he said in the shrill voice of a little boy, like a sneer coming from the weathered face and black eyes of a grown man.

"Don't shout, Mommino, everyone's asleep," Papandrè scolded. Mommino shrugged, resigned to his voice.

Totò Asaro began to resume his tale. Papandrè stopped him, squeezing his knee with a heavy hand. "I get it, Totò, I get it. It's not you I'm worried about." And he looked questioningly at Mommino. Mommino studied the two men waiting for him to speak.

"They came to my house,..." he began, in his deafening high-pitched shriek. Papandrè gasped and motioned with his left hand to make him lower his voice.

"They came to my house,..." Mommino began again, struck by a sudden and severe hoarseness which rendered his speech barely audible. "They took me to the station. Totò had said that I was here too and I explained that I happened to be in the piazza when they were shooting, that I had seen a short man, not too short, like me, almost like me, thin build, thin, yes, skinny, like me, in black, like me, wearing a beret, this guy was running in the piazza and I shouted, trying to keep him from getting away, *stop him stop him stop him.*"

His voice had turned shrill again. Papandrè gasped loudly. Mommino Falletta started once more, hoarsely: "And the chief was asking questions I was expecting but wasn't supposed to act like I was expecting like why did I come here it was because everyone knows the mayor was like a brother to you, and right here in front of the door I ran into Totò, and we heard all those voices coming from inside a residence not far away and this same guy Totò Asaro told me that the residence is inhabited by someone named Vincenzo Picipò who I don't know, just his face is familiar, not having any ties of friendship or association..."

"I'm tired. I get tired listening to you, Mommino." Papandrè let out a sigh which made the lightbulb overhead sway. Mommino dropped his eyes, humiliated. He hunched his shoulders.

The room fell silent. From somewhere in the house came the faint ticking of a clock. Papandrè was gasping for breath. The air was close. Mommino bent down again to pick up the cigarette stubs. Papandrè burst out in breath and words: "Leave the cigarettes."

Mommino Falletta dropped the butts.

Now Papandrè tried to smile, showing his little teeth.

"Mommino, I understand we're nervous, but we don't need to worry."

"No, we don't need to worry," added Totò Asaro.

"We don't need to worry. This thing is moving along like it's supposed to. You gave your statement, you've done your duty. It's like embroidery, one stitch at a time, one stitch at a time. Have you ever seen the women sitting in their doorways doing embroidery, Mommino?"

"Yes, Papandrè."

"And this is good. One stitch at a time. Each one looks separate. You don't understand what good are those threads they're pulling on over here and over there, and little by little the embroidery takes shape."

"Sure, Papandrè."

"Good boys. An hour ago the carabinieri came to get Hundred-Ten. Were you still at the station?"

Totò Asaro and Mommino Falletta looked at each other. Totò spoke. "Me, they sent home after taking my statement. Mommino stayed."

Papandrè pointed to the empty chair next to him.

"Come over here, Mommo, so I can hear you better."

Mommino moved from his place in front of Papandrè and sat down at his left. A fat hand fell on his knee.

"You saw him?"

"They showed him to me," whispered Mommino.

"And..."

"There were two others, guys I know because they're from around here, but in the lineup I only pointed to Picipò whose height was the height of the killer and also the suit matched the one worn by Picipò who I knew from before though without any friendship or association."

"You said it was him?"

"No, I said it looked like him."

"And this is good...get it, Totò?"

6

The bitter taste rose from corporal Nanìa's stomach and burned his throat. The train ride, the lack of sleep, the gluttony of the past few days had upset his digestion. He couldn't figure out if it was better to eat or fast. All he knew was that the queasiness was climbing furiously from his stomach to his head.

"You look pale, corporal. Are you sure you're all right?"

"Yes chief, I'm fine."

And that fucking sergeant wouldn't stop smoking. Since nine at night, he'd sucked down a whole pack of Camels. And he was about to open another. Those cigarettes must be eating up his paycheck, or maybe he had a whore for a sister, paid in packs of "Americans."

"Come on, Corporal, we're almost done," said the chief. "Go call the other witness, what's his name, Spoto Puleo."

Sergeant Di Dio waited until the corporal was already at the door.

"Chief, don't you think we should go over Collura's statement again?"

Perez turned towards the sergeant, stunned, afraid the man had caught onto the game. Not Corporal Nanìa, certainly — he was an idiot to begin with, and food poisoning had rendered him immune to the already faint possibility of cerebral activity. But Sergeant Di Dio was another matter. To his usual lazy and obtuse nature was sometimes added a perverse contrariness.

Nanìa, hovering in the doorway: "What should I do, Chief, should I call Spoto Puleo?"

Chief Perez narrowed his eyes at the corporal, then again at the sergeant sitting in a corner of the room, his uniform unbuttoned, another cigarette held, oddly, between his ring and little fingers.

"Sergeant, open the window. How can you smoke so much?..."

Di Dio, rising and moving slowly, obeyed. The rain had stopped. The cool air didn't manage to disperse the thick smoke right away. The sergeant went back to his seat.

"Yes, we'll go over Collura's statement," said the chief, picking up two sheets of carbon paper.

The sergeant feigned disinterest, shifting his cigarette's position, inserting it between his middle and ring fingers as the chief watched him.

"It's so my fingers don't turn yellow. Sometimes I even smoke with my left hand, that way the tar gets distributed across both hands, and you don't see it," explained Di Dio.

Chief Perez appeared thunderstruck, as if by pure chance he'd learned the Three Secrets of Fátima. And just as quickly, his face resumed its usual tired and overburdened look, its usual fogged eyes.

"So, the statement by Collura, Enrico, where does it start, ah, here it is...around 7:45 p.m....we were...okay, let's begin."

"Chief, do I call Spoto Puleo?"

"Sit down, Corporal, sit down. I'll tell you when to call him."

Nanìa plopped back behind the typewriter. He let himself slip down until he was hidden from the chief, leaned his head against the wall and let his eyes close a little.

"Wasted night," he thought. He was belching softly, without being heard, concentrating on his mysterious intestinal upheavals, the only real focus of his interest, above that of the dead man, of the killer, and of the investigation, which actually was in good order. Unlike his stomach.

"Here we go," said Perez, settling in his chair to read out loud the statement signed three hours earlier by Enrico Collura. "At 7:45 p.m. I was accompanying the mayor, Baldassare Farrauto, along Corso Garibaldi, exchanging some words. Shortly thereafter we were stopped by one Vincenzo Picipò, father unknown, also called Hundred-Ten, who, behaving like a mafioso, approached the mayor asking for a reason why he hadn't been given work in the sulfur mine or doing road repair. Moreover, he said that others were working while he was getting screwed and left without a job. Mr. Farrauto replied that his accusations had no basis in reality and in an irritated manner asked him to come and talk the following day. Mr. Picipò however, still acting like a bully, told him he wanted to settle the matter immediately."

"...settle the matter immediately," repeated Di Dio.

The chief looked up. "That's what it says."

The sergeant nodded, to show that he understood the double meaning of the phrase. But there was no double meaning. The chief felt comforted by this. The sergeant was an asshole, and maybe he'd never catch on.

"Let's go on...he told him that he wanted to settle the matter immediately. At this point" — and here the chief raised his voice, shaking Nanìa out of his torpor — "At this point I grabbed Picipò by the arm, requesting him to leave, but since he continued assaulting Mr. Farrauto with his nonsense, I led him over by the church, inviting him once more to go home. Mr. Picipò, animated by the wine he had ingested, interpreted my conciliatory behavior as if I were trying to defend Mr. Farrauto, telling me that if the mayor didn't give him satisfaction, he'd get it from me. Angered, I administered two slaps to Picipò, and it was due to the intervention of some passersby that it went no further..."

"...for the moment," interrupted the sergeant.

"Sergeant, that business, that fight, went no further. There's a full stop here. Please, let me finish."

"Excuse me, Chief."

"So...where were we? Ah, then Collura goes back to the piazza, etcetera etcetera, finds Mr. Farrauto...who asks him...Mr. Collura responds that it was nothing...in short, they continue walking in the piazza...here we are: around 8:20 p.m., Mr. Farrauto said goodbye and having called over the town clerk, Angelo Spoto Puleo, turned towards the street to go home. Period. I and others, among whom, etcetera etcetera, stayed behind to talk, when we heard shooting. Period. There followed a massive flight of persons from the piazza, which initially confused us. Period," and again Perez looked at the sergeant to cut off any possible interruption. "Next we ran towards the scene of the crime and discovered the corpse of Mr. Farrauto lying on the ground, soaked in blood. Period. I saw many persons fleeing, but due to the darkness I was unable to recognize them. Period. I have nothing further to add and in affirmation of the above, I, the undersigned, Enrico Collura, etcetera etcetera."

"Good," said the sergeant.

At that word, the chief realized that the sergeant, as on other and repeated occasions, understood nothing, and if he had played the part, it was only to puff himself up and to keep on breaking balls, as on other and repeated occasions.

Perez almost shouted: "Nanìa, call the witness! Wake up!"

The new witness had a head shining with oil, his hair combed back, and a yellow-toothed smile that stretched only his mouth, leaving his eyes cold and motionless.

The chief was getting pushy and excited. He sensed that the investigation was already a sharpened blade, and this man would give him the handle to grasp it with.

"All right, Spoto Puleo. You're the town clerk. Nanìa, start taking this down. Signor Spoto, you know you have to tell the truth, since you're here as a witness..."

The man spoke in a deep, decisive voice. "I know the procedure, Chief. You ask the questions, and I answer."

Nanìa was taking dictation without understanding a single word that flew from the keys. The food poisoning or the hunger, whichever it was, pounded furiously at his temples. It pounded as furiously as Nanìa pounded the keys in recording Spoto Puleo's statement. The corporal had no idea that the statement he was recording was the key to the entire investigation. Any moral queasiness he felt on this occasion was dulled by an inability to comprehend, which always rendered him and always would render him immune to life, even when he was in the best of health. The words uttered by the witness and repeated by the chief issued from the fingers of Corporal Nanìa, safely armored within his illness.

"In the year nineteen hundred forty-four, on the 7th day of the month of November, in the office of the aforementioned station, time 1:30 a.m. Here present before the below-signed officers of the judicial police is the above-referenced Angelo Spoto Puleo, who, being duly questioned, declares...type, Nanìa, type!" said the chief.

Spoto Puleo began: "At about 8:20 p.m. on the evening of the 6th of November, I was beckoned by the mayor, Farrauto Baldassare, to accompany him home, as I did every evening. Together we started down the Corso in order to reach Via Asaro. In front of the Cacioppo Café there were many groups of people, and we continued on our way, pushing through the crowd. At a certain point we separated in order to go around and move past a man who had stopped, dressed in black, with a dark beret, of rather short stature, with his back to us. Having gone some meters beyond him and rejoining the mayor, I heard a loud bang behind me and felt a blast and noticed the acrid odor of gunpowder..."

"Type, Corporal, type!"

"I was dazed by the shot, since it was fired at a very short distance from me, and I saw the mayor, Baldassare Farrauto, fall to the ground. When I recovered my senses a moment later, I saw people fleeing down the streets that branch out from this spot in all directions, but I didn't know any of them. Next, I took refuge in the Cacioppo Café where, barely conscious, I was given a chair and a glass of water."

Nanìa, without intending or wanting to, was also the coauthor of a brief but critical sequence of "In Response to Questions":

> *I.R.Q. — I didn't clearly recognize the man we passed, but I do not exclude the possibility of his having been Vincenzo Picipò, father unknown, also called Hundred-Ten, because the man was dressed in black, with a dark beret, of short stature and slender build, all characteristics that fully correspond to those of Picipò.*

> *I.R.Q. — There existed old grudges between Baldassare Farrauto and Vincenzo Picipò, due to which they shared a deadly hatred of each other.*

> *I.R.Q. — I further recall that Farrauto once had an animated discussion with Picipò in the mayor's office, because the latter arrogantly demanded that the mayor give him social assistance without working for it. Furthermore, Farrauto had confessed to me that it was Vincenzo Picipò who, in exchange for leaving the mayor alone, had gotten him involved some years before in criminal activity, influencing certain junior officers of the carabinieri for whom Picipò was an informant. I have nothing further to add, and in affirmation of the above, I sign myself, Angelo Spoto Puleo.*

DAY

1

The cold wind was whipping down the throat of the Funnuto Pass, right off Monte Cammarata. It had swept away the clouds of the night before. But the roads were still wet.

Lieutenant Adano shivered. He hadn't brought his overcoat, since he hadn't needed to wear it yet in Naples. He'd hoped that Sicily would be warm.

"*Veri cold, tudei,*" said Semino.

"Yeah,..." said the lieutenant, trembling.

They were going down the road past the cemetery, towards the sulfur mine. The jeep brushed past men on the back of a mule, a goat tied behind and a dog trotting nearby, sniffing the wet grass. Other men, on foot, were going back up towards the town.

"Miners, *thei work andergraund,* under the mountains, Lieutenant. In the mines you work even at night, because down there it's *blackout*, never day, never any stars."

The stars. The moon. Adano recalled something by Pirandello — he couldn't help it — from one of his stories. The darkness of the mine, the bright moon on coming out of the tunnel, a boy's exhaustion. What was it called?

Along the road there were two little boys with bare legs, brothers maybe, wearing enormous jackets, old grownups' jackets. Looking wide-eyed at the jeep, they greeted it with upturned palms. The lieutenant caught their words: "*Mii, sono tornati gli americani.*" *Fuuck, the Americans are back.* But they were already far behind.

The road was now immersed in a runoff of thick, yellowish, sulfurous water.

"*Acqua di santi*, holy water, good for stomach problems," noted Semino.

Shuddering, Adano was mesmerized by the fetid stream, asking himself if he could ever drink from it. More like water from hell.

The hills up ahead were red and yellow. Columns of smoke rose briefly into the clear sky, quickly dispersed by the wind.

"Ovens. The sulfur ore is melted down inside. Nothing grows around here, the fumes from the mines eat away everything," explained Semino, downshifting as they climbed.

The Iacuzzo Pietrebianche Mine could not have been further from any idea Adano might have had of an industrial operation. A levelled yard of rust-colored gravel, two low mounds of chalk, perhaps deposited by the machinery. Three two-wheeled mule carts were stopped next to a rectangular pile. Getting closer, Adano realized that it was made of blocks of sulfur, stacked on top of each other. The entrance to the mine was a kind of cave, not large, without any allure or mystery. A dark hole in the side of the hill.

It was silent. Semino pulled up to one of the two warehouses and shut off the engine. Only the screeching of a crow, far off.

A man in coat and tie came out of the building.

"*Qui non si puo stare*," he shouted. *You can't stay here.*

"We have to talk,..." Adano began.

"No, look, you can't stay here." The man kept his hands on the jeep door to prevent the lieutenant from getting out.

"I have to speak to the owner," Adano ventured.

"The owner's not here. I'm the bookkeeper, but I can't tell you anything. What's your business?"

"You've got some trucks here?"

The accountant smiled. He pointed to the carts and the cart drivers who were loading blocks of sulfur.

"If that's what you want to call them…"

"Look, I'm an American officer. I need…"

"Listen to me. I'm not interested in who you are, with all respect. But outsiders can't be here, I can't take responsibility for that. Talk to Signor Farrauto. You'll find him at city hall, he's the mayor. He operates the mine…"

"Maybe you don't know it yet, but the mayor was killed last night."

The accountant's brows furrowed. Then he smiled: "What are you talking about?"

"Last night, in the piazza, they shot him."

The man abruptly turned and quickened his pace towards the warehouse. Reaching the entrance, he turned back. "Go away, you can't stay here, it's forbidden. You have to go away now," he shouted.

He stood still in the doorway until the jeep was back on the road.

Semino was quiet. He thought it would be better to leave town as soon as possible. Lieutenant Adano was trying to figure out who could give him an answer, *any* answer, so he could close the case and leave, go back to Palermo, stop there for a few days, gaze in awe at the Arab-Norman Cuba Palace, visit the cathedral, go up Montepellegrino all the way to Monreale. In short, retrace the steps of Goethe in the land where the lemon trees bloom.

"Semino, let's go see the carabinieri."

"What for, Signor Lieutenant?"

"Let's go, maybe we'll catch the chief there."

"It's better to leave the carabinieri alone." Semino had not forgotten that under the reign of the anti-mafia crusader Mori, he'd been held for six days. By those carabinieri. He had no love for them.

Past the cemetery, beyond the curve, in the middle of the road, a woman. She was in tears, dragging three little boys behind her. The two smallest were crying and one was seized with coughing. The oldest was following his mother and those who appeared to be his brothers with a grave, almost ashamed face.

The woman threw herself to the side of the road to avoid the jeep. She yanked the littlest one after her, making him fall down in front of the wheel of the car, which Semino had stopped. Adano jumped out, afraid the child had been hit.

The little boy had scraped his knees, nothing serious. The coughing shook him harder now, from within. His mother gave him a slap: "Aren't we in enough trouble already?"

The woman shrank back, noticing Adano's uniform. She was terrified, shaken.

"Signora, what's happened to the boy?"

"*Niente, niente.*" *Nothing.* The wind was turning colder. Adano got back in the jeep. "Can I help?"

No response. Semino put the jeep in gear. The lieutenant caught a movement — the woman, leaving her children on the side of the road, was now approaching the car.

"You're American?"

The lieutenant said yes with his head, like the Sicilians.

"My husband worked with the Americans. Help me, sir. We have no one." She pointed to her children. Semino was staring straight ahead, expressionless.

"What can I do, Signora?"

"They took my husband last night. But I swear before the Madonna of the Mountain, he didn't kill the mayor. Help me. You're American, sir. The Americans have always helped us."

2

Celery, two bunches. And potatoes — a kilo, a kilo and a half. Two lemons. A little parsley. That's it.

The judge usually left his office after midday, stopped by Angelina's shop, chatted a bit, bought fruit and vegetables, and then went to the gentleman's club. He would read *The Daily Sicilian* for half an hour and go home at a quarter to one. Upon leaving the club, he almost always turned back after a few dozen meters, having forgotten the groceries he'd left with the waiter.

With the two bunches of celery, a kilo and a half of potatoes, two lemons and some parsley wrapped in a sheet of paper, he crossed the piazza. He passed in front of the Cacioppo Café but kept to the opposite sidewalk, avoiding the spot where the mayor's corpse had lain until dawn.

On his usual corner, a man was squatting next to a basket full of white snails, the kind for cooking in broth with potatoes. He bought almost two kilos, even though his wife didn't eat them. They put her off, more because of the disgusting pleasure of cooking them and sucking them out one by one, than for their flesh. But the judge found them delicious.

Someone greeted him from the opposite sidewalk. He responded with calculated reserve. At that hour only produce merchants and the idle loafed about the piazza. Most were without work and in the judge's view would never find any, having no wish to.

The crack of billiard balls, their faint rumble on the green felt, chalk being rubbed onto the ends of the cues: these same sounds recurred each day, with imperceptible variations, as he entered the club. The lawyer Giangreco,

Ignazio Mulè, and Professor Nicolò Brucculeri would be locked in fierce competition. From ten in the morning until one in the afternoon they vied with each other at billiards. In the afternoons, from five to eight (with a one-hour delay in summer), they lost themselves in endless card games.

Today, the judge was surprised. The club was silent. No rumble of balls, no squeaking of chalk. Handing over his groceries, he gave the waiter a questioning look.

"No games today. Mourning for the mayor."

"Ah,..." the judge approved. The mayor hadn't belonged to the club, but all of its members held a kind of formal (and formal only) respect for his duly constituted authority.

He proceeded, the waiter hovering behind him. "They're expecting you."

This was disquieting, but it was too late to turn back.

In the salon they greeted the judge's arrival by raising their eyes from their newspapers with ostentatious indifference and staring.

He took a copy of the newspaper, spied an armchair by the window, and tried to conceal himself behind the sheets of printed paper. He read distractedly. A Liberal rally in Cattolica Eraclea. Palermo: Finocchiaro Aprile leads a demonstration of Sicilian separatists. Three bandits arrested in the countryside near Misilmeri. He paused at some news from Agrigento: in recent days unknown thieves had absconded with a first-class radio set from the social club at Porto Empedocleo. It was valued at about 60,000 lire, or thirty-two packs of American cigarettes. In the initial investigation conducted by the forces of public safety, some of the club's waiters were detained. But on the following day the aforementioned radio was discovered near the police station, abandoned by thieves who evidently feared having their homes searched. The case was being actively pursued.

He lowered the paper. All eyes were on him.

"Terrible misfortune," sighed Mulè. A real-estate dealer, he owned land but had personally never farmed.

"And to think that I ran into him yesterday afternoon. We said hello, cordially, like always," said Professor Brucculeri. "*O tempora o mores....*"

Silence.

They were waiting for the judge to speak, to furnish some bit of official news beyond the crop of homegrown truths that started sprouting a few minutes after the gunshot.

Brucculeri and Mulè, with a quick, simultaneous raising of eyebrows, encouraged the lawyer Giangreco, in recognition of his jurisprudential competence.

"In this particular case," — and here Giangreco cleared his throat — "if the findings of the authorities are borne out, and, specifically, if those relating to Picipò, better known as Hundred-Ten, are confirmed by evidence and testimony..."

"Hundred-Ten is fucked," Mulè interrupted.

"That is your conclusion," resumed the lawyer. "Only the honorable judge can assure us, as far as his official duties permit, what positive or negative results may have emerged with respect to Picipò, who is however in custody. Right?"

The judge squirmed in his armchair. He had to toss these ravenous hounds something to chew on. And perhaps he could eke out something in return: The dark, cloudy motivations, the reversals and fractures of a game being played without him. With any luck, once the part of the investigation that was nominally under his jurisdiction was completed, the game would actually be decided in the higher Court of Assizes, thereby relieving him of any responsibility, moral or judicial, and of any conceivable danger.

"You understand that this is all subject to the strictest rules of confidentiality,..." the judge began.

"Of course."

"Of course."

"Of course." But they were already relishing the indiscretion.

"I cannot hide the fact," the judge continued in a low voice, "that there are several witnesses, as you well know. Two who had gone to the home of Andrea Restivo Maranella..."

"Papandrè,..." clarified Mulè.

"Exactly. Two who had gone to warn him, immediately after the crime, well aware of the ties between the mayor and Restivo Maranella, ties of kinship and brotherly affection."

"Brotherly affection," emphasized the lawyer Giangreco. The judge flattered himself for having caught the insinuation.

"Well then. The two witnesses, while standing in the doorway waiting to be admitted, overheard, coming from the residence of Picipò, which stands not far from that of Restivo Maranella, desperate cries..."

"Desperate?" asked Professor Brucculeri.

"Desperate, professor, that's how they were described by the two witnesses, whose names I naturally cannot reveal..."

"Totò Asaro," Giangreco whispered to Mulè.

"And Mommino Falletta," rejoined Mulè.

"So you say," the judge continued. "In any case, as our attorney Giangreco has in part already demonstrated, from the statement of Enrico Collura — and I can speak this name because it's no mystery, an intimate friend of the mayor's — a dispute emerges between the mayor and Picipò, resurfacing less than an hour before the homicide. And so, the motive."

"The slaps," said Mulè, turning to the lawyer Giangreco, disappointed because none of this was news to anyone.

"But it was Collura who slapped Picipò, not the mayor,..." Professor Brucculeri pointed out.

"Professor, professor." The lawyer Giangreco generously condescended to share the full benefit of his legalistic expertise. "Yes, it was Collura who did the slapping, but it was owing to a verbal offense aimed at the mayor, and in response to same. Therefore, Picipò would have taken the slaps on behalf of and in the name of the mayor. The motive, as you see, fits."

"And finally, the eyewitness," the judge casually let slip.

"Eyewitness?"

"Eyewitness, precisely. In this case, the eye belonging to the witness Spoto Puleo, the town clerk who regularly accompanied the mayor on his way home. He was able to recognize Picipò as the short man of slender build, wearing a dark suit, who would have shot the mayor."

This made them thoughtful, suspended in the gravity of the moment.

The lawyer Giangreco broke the silence. "He's fucked. Given that, I wouldn't in good conscience care to defend Hundred-Ten." Everyone nodded. They knew that neither Hundred-Ten nor anyone else would resort to the lawyer Giangreco. Thirteen years earlier, he had uttered his first and last courtroom speech, which might be boiled down to the legal principle "silence is the best defense." His client was sentenced to the maximum penalty under the law, plus extra for aggravating circumstances.

"Of course, Picipò did have an alibi."

Giangreco, Brucculeri, and Mulè leapt at these words from the judge.

"Alibi?"

"Weak perhaps, but still an alibi. Two neighbor women, paying a visit to Hundred-Ten's wife, saw him come home before eight p.m. with bruises on his face, and they saw him get ready for bed, at which point they left to avoid further aggravating Picipò, who was visibly upset."

"That changes everything," exclaimed the lawyer Giangreco.

"Well, gentlemen, it's getting late. I must bid you farewell." The judge got up from his armchair. It was fifteen minutes to one. "I don't think I need to ask for your confidentiality — I'm aware of your discretion," he said, taking his leave. He was followed out by the waiter, trying to give him back his bundle of groceries.

The lawyer Giangreco paced the salon in long steps. "Alibi. He calls this an alibi?"

"Maybe they haven't told the judge everything," suggested Professor Brucculeri.

"In my opinion, they haven't told him shit," mused Mulè.

"But even *we* know this alibi is worthless, and even we know there's another witness against him." The lawyer Giangreco was waving his arms.

"Papandrè's relative?" asked the professor.

"Precisely, professor, precisely. With that testimony they'll put a gravestone over Hundred-Ten."

"And the judge, why doesn't he know anything?"

"Maybe he's a bit of an asshole."

"Except for the maybe."

3

"This is good. Repeat it once more."

"Once more?"

"Once more, once more."

"Alright..."

"Sure you don't want to eat?" said Papandrè, taking another *costoletta di castrato* from the platter.

"No thank you," said the young man sitting across from him, his hands resting on the bare, unset half of the table. "It was just after eight..."

"Let's try to be more precise, Nicolò."

"It was five after eight or maybe seven after, because I had just looked at my watch..."

"And this is good,..." grunted Papandrè, tearing off the bone what little meat there was with his teeth.

"I was going home, when ahead of me, at a distance of about eight meters, also on Via Giuseppe Verdi, I noticed a woman who was walking rather hurriedly towards the piazza."

"A glass of wine?"

"That I'll have, with pleasure."

Papandrè poured a glass of red wine. Pressing his belly against the table, he pushed it towards the young man sitting opposite. "Let's continue."

"Right. I noticed that the woman knocked on the door of a house, still on Via Giuseppe Verdi, but without waiting for it to open she kept walking along at the same pace..."

"Towards the piazza..."

"Yes, towards the piazza. I had the impression that something odd was going on, so when I got to my house, on the same Via Verdi, I asked Signorina Graziella Gesafatti, who lives across from me and who happened to be standing in the doorway of her house, who that woman was —she must have seen her too. Signorina Gesafatti responded that it was Maria Merulla, the wife of Hundred-Ten, the same lady..."

"The same lady,..." Papandrè echoed in emphasis.

"The same lady who, very worried, was going around saying out loud to herself, 'Where can I find him at this hour, where can I find him at this hour?' We both understood, I and Signorina Gesafatti, that something unusual was going on, for which reason we decided to retire to our respective homes."

"And you went to bed?"

"Yes."

"And...?"

"And what?"

"Nicolò, are you retarded?"

"Ah yes...the next morning..."

"When you woke up..."

"When I woke up and learned that the mayor had been killed, I thought back on the episode of the night before and concluded that the likely murderer was Hundred-Ten."

"And you didn't know anything else, right?" Papandrè raised high a finger, like a prophet invoking a heavenly threat.

"Nothing. I didn't know anything about the argument the mayor had had the night before with Hundred-Ten, because if I'd known..."

"If you'd known,..." Papandrè's eyes became slits.

"...if I'd known, it would have further confirmed my suspicions, and the logical connection I'd established between the murder and the previous night's episode involving the wife would have been even stronger."

"And this is good," exclaimed Papandrè. "Bravo. You talk liked a printed page. Signorina Graziella can confirm this, right?"

Young Nicolò smiled suggestively. "Signorina Graziella will confirm this. She certainly will."

"And you and Signorina Graziella?..." Papandrè finished the question with a gesture.

"Things happen,..." smiled Nicolò.

"And this is good."

"You do what you can."

"Bravo. Go over it for me once more."

"Once more?"

"Once more."

"But when do I need to go to the police station?"

"Don't worry about it. They'll come looking for you."

"They who?"

"The carabinieri, idiot."

"And why are they looking for me?"

"Because someone's told them you know something, and maybe, after some hesitation, you'll tell the carabinieri."

"Then I'll go home and wait."

"Yes...but first, let's go over everything."

"From the beginning?"

"From the beginning."

"It was 8:05 p.m. because I checked my watch when I got home, like always..."

"And this is good."

4

"Chief, what do I tell the American? Do I make him wait?"

Irritated, the chief roused himself from the pile of statements made overnight, which he'd been reading and re-reading. His eyes were still red from sleeplessness and rage. He was close to completing an investigation that was already sufficient to keep Hundred-Ten in jail. But something more was needed, and Chief Perez didn't know where to find it.

"Ah, the American. So what does he want?"

For Corporal Nanìa, two hours of uneasy, anxious sleep had not been enough to overcome his indigestion. If anything, it had been aggravated by the premonitions that always accompanied his gastric episodes, filling him with a terrible dread of dying.

"He says he wants to speak with you personally."

"In American?"

"No, he speaks Italian."

The chief studied Nanìa. He sensed that the lieutenant was bringing him aggravation. American aggravation, but still aggravation. "Corporal, your face could make someone ill, speaking with respect. The face of a corpse."

Nanìa didn't respond, apart from furtively grabbing his crotch in the doorway of the chief's office to ward off bad luck.

"My stomach. The usual problem."

"Then go to the pharmacy, get something for it. I can't tell you to go home and rest, you see how we're stretched... but take something so you don't die in the line of duty."

Nanìa planned on grabbing himself with greater and more elaborate care, in a private place. "So should I let the American in?"

"Let him in."

Nanìa went to the station's waiting room, taking advantage of those five steps to energetically ward off the two funereal allusions. "*Prego*, Lieutenant, the chief is waiting for you."

Then the corporal got his cap, buckled on his white shoulder strap, and left for the pharmacy. He found Sergeant Di Dio in front of the station, leaning on the American's jeep. He was joking and laughing with the lieutenant's driver, trying to wangle himself some packs of cigarettes. He was fresh as a rose and still doing nothing, as he'd done his entire life. Nanìa mentally wished he'd drop dead. His indigestion generally intensified his standing hatred for the sergeant.

The chief got to his feet — the American was an officer after all, and Perez was merely a non-commissioned maresciallo. Perez was well aware that his own Fascist predecessor had avoided being sent to a POW camp in North Africa after the Allied landing only by sheer luck. Luck, and the intervention of certain friends.

The station stank of smoke and nicotine. Adano stood looking at the crucifix behind the chief's back. Something was missing from the wall: the portrait of America's new ally, King Vittorio Emanuele III.

He pointed this out to Perez. The chief abruptly turned around, stunned by this observation. He turned back to Adano. "It's not there."

"No, it's not."

"It's around here somewhere, though. Maybe in the sergeant's office."

"Maybe."

Chief Perez was convinced that this American was a ballbreaker. He was prepared to treat him as best he could, and as best he could, to get rid of him.

"Lieutenant, can I do something for you?"

"I understand it's not a good time, you have a lot to do..."

"Well..."

"I heard about the mayor..."

"Terrible. But we already have the murderer in custody."

"Signor Picipò, also known as Hundred-Ten."

Perez examined Adano with eyes reddened by sleeplessness and rage. He was convinced: the American was a ballbreaker. "You understand that the investigation is still under way, but since you're an officer from a nation that's our friend and ally, not to mention the occupying force until a few months ago, I can confirm it. Yes, Signor Picipò is under arrest."

"Chief, I'm not here to do your job, which I'm sure you're doing quite well..."

Perez seemed to detect a trace of irony, but he let the lieutenant continue.

"But I have some information that might turn out to be useful for you. Just like you might be able to help me in the little investigation that my commanding officer assigned to me regarding the disappearance of some trucks, property of the allied military administration, hijacked at gunpoint between September 1943 and June of this year on the road between town and the Iacuzzo Pietrebianche Mine."

The chief took his time. "Information?"

Adano opened his leather portfolio and pulled out some papers. "Yes, information regarding Baldassare Farrauto. From some of our reports, not secret, but filed by our Civil Affairs officers subsequent to his appointment as mayor, some interesting facts emerge. Like here, I see that Farrauto was considered a business partner, in this same Iacuzzo

Pietrebianche Mine, of Calò Vizzini, believed to be the mafia capo of the Agrigento–Caltanisetta mining region. And from this same document, it turns out that recently he'd been engaged in political activity with the separatist movement. Look here. On June 4th 1944, five months ago, he participated in the assembly of town and regional representatives in Palermo, organized by the mayor, Lucio Tasca. Mayors were there from all over Sicily, including this Vizzini, who was standing in for the mayor of Villalba, Giuseppe Genco Russo, and for the mayor of Mussomeli. In other words, men of some importance, men who'd spent years in jail, and not just for being anti-Fascist. Now, I think that the homicide — though I don't know how far the investigation's gone — could well have some more complex causes tied to the mayor's various business interests..."

Adano had kept his eyes on his papers, but in holding them out to the chief, he found the man shrinking back in his chair, almost pressing against the wall. He was shaking his head. The lieutenant tried to insist. "Please, take a look at these documents, if you would."

The chief was shaking, his eyes turning redder. Adano explained, "Of course, I can't let you keep them. But surely there are useful findings..."

Only then did Perez rest his hands on the desk. Slowly, with his full weight, starting at his waist, he rose up. "Useful?" he whispered.

"What did you say?" asked Adano, perplexed.

"But how do you know what information is useful? You come here to show me some documents, you talk to me of things we already know and which we have verified time and time again, you invent theories which don't exist in heaven or on earth. Do you have anything specific to say about this homicide?"

"No, nothing really specific..."

"Then don't say anything. If you can give me specifics, and I mean *specifics*, I'll take your statement and you'll officially turn over those documents. And you don't turn them over to me, but to the judge. Otherwise, tell me what you need, and I'll see if I can help you..."

Chief Perez's eyes were now red only from anger. His tone was agitated. He was aware of it and aware of the bars on the American's collar. Adano was an officer, after all. Perez remained standing.

"Nanìa! Corporal Nanìa!..." he shouted towards the doorway. Then he turned to Adano. "You'd like to know about some stolen trucks, you said. Do you know how many stolen animals, stolen bushels of grain, home burglaries, armed train robberies, how much livestock rustling, extortion, kidnapping goes on in this town?"

He turned to a wooden cabinet and opened it. It was overflowing with papers. "Nanìa! Corporal Nanìa!..." he shouted again towards the doorway. He pulled bundles of statements from the cabinet. He flung them furiously on his desk.

"Livestock rustling, breaking and entering, assault, assault, insulting a public official, assault with a deadly weapon, assault with a deadly weapon, homicide, livestock rustling, more rustling, theft, armed kidnapping, armed kidnapping, homicide, homicide, homicide...Nanìaaaaaa!"

The sergeant's face appeared in the partly opened doorway. "The corporal's out. Did you call, Chief?"

"Yes, I called. Where's Nanìa? Well, *you're* here. Look, take these statements, let the lieutenant have a look. Maybe something *useful* will turn up." He loaded down the sergeant with the papers.

Adano had fallen silent. The chief pointed to Di Dio. "Go on, Lieutenant, go with the sergeant. You might even find your trucks in these statements. But they're all accusations against unknown suspects, they're all charges with no trials and no criminals, because we never have any criminals around here."

"*Almost* never," Adano found the courage to say.

"And when we find them, we hold them tight. We practically become friends."

Lieutenant Adano followed the sergeant as he staggered to the other office, his arms loaded with papers and an American cigarette dangling from his lips.

The chief, left alone, let himself drop down into his chair. He unbuttoned his uniform, gasping. "We make friends with the criminals," he thought again, out loud. The door opened.

It was Nanìa, paler than ever. "Nanìa, I've been calling you for half an hour. Where have you been?"

"To the pharmacy, Chief, like you told me."

"Ah, true. Feel better now?"

"A little...but in the pharmacy, I ran into Signorina Rosina Giglio, Signor Restivo Maranella's cousin."

"And?"

"She told me that Signorina Gesafatti told her in church today about seeing Hundred-Ten's wife the other evening, just before the crime, running down the street looking for her husband and repeating 'Where can I find him at this hour? Where can I find him at this hour?'"

The chief gave thanks to heaven. God, or someone on His behalf, had sent him what he needed. He jumped to his feet, buttoning up his uniform. "Nanìa, we're going to Signorina Gesafatti's."

"Now?"

"Immediately."

Nanìa prepared to leave. The chief's voice stopped him. "Nanìa, where's the king?"

The corporal instinctively snapped to attention. "In Rome, I believe."

"Nanìa, when you're ill you're stupider than usual. The picture, the *picture* of the king, where did it go?"

5

"Shameless, shameless, shameless."

"*Shhh*, she might hear you."

"She *better* hear me. I want her to. But that one never even blushes."

"Quiet, for pity's sake. Have respect for the dead," whispered Concettina Sardo, a gossip herself, but pious and forgiving.

Donna Adelina Farrauto was too aggrieved to put aside her indignation over the presence — in the same house, before the body of her poor brother, slaughtered like a rabid dog — of that shameless Lucina Saccomanda, Baldassare's mistress when he was alive, suffered and tolerated through gritted teeth only for the sake of peace. And out of fear of the brother on whom the entire existence of the spinster Donna Adelina depended.

But now, with Baldassare dead — rest his soul — there was no longer any reason for "that one" to stay, playing the mistress of the grand palazzo, while Donna Adelina had to content herself with a little apartment to one side — with all the comforts and conveniences, but still an apartment.

"Shameless, shameless, shameless," Donna Adelina repeated.

Lucina Saccomanda couldn't hear. She was in another room. From the moment the dead man entered the house, the two women had not crossed paths. They took turns in the visitation room, each one taking advantage of the other's absences, imposed by basic bodily needs, irrepressible in spite of such grief.

And when one of them won the place of honor on the right side of the casket, from which the mayor continued to rule — not even death, nor the strip of white cloth tied around his head, could soften his sneering arrogance — hours and dozens of quarter-hour strikes of the pendulum clock would have to pass, and infinite shufflings of dragged feet and whispers of condolences and bursts of tears and heartrending sighs and hugs from embarrassed visitors, before she abandoned her post, well aware that the other would reoccupy it in order to reclaim the dead man, who was torn between one love legitimate and brotherly and another with equal claims, albeit illicit.

The reason the mayor had never wanted to marry, despite living with Lucina Saccomanda for thirteen years, was one of those mysteries which no one had ever summoned the courage to ask Baldassare Farrauto to explain, not even those who accompanied him on his walks every evening through the piazza or on his more mysterious travels out of town on business.

Except once. A priest, paternally and as a Christian — and on the strength of a distant and comradely sharing of a desk at the elementary school they had attended in the 80's — had invited him to rectify his situation before God. The mayor replied, "Lucina loves me, but she has a past."

There was no trace of that past in the town, because Lucina came from far away, a port city, and as such lent herself to tales of fantasy and sexual filth set among the slums of the Mediterranean, a sea which many in the town had never seen, despite the fact that it was less than thirty kilometers away. Of course, no one knew why Baldassare Farrauto had returned with a woman from such a place — but at least he'd waited until after the death of his mother, who would never have tolerated the sharing of her adored only male child.

Donna Adelina could not ask of her brother what their mother had demanded, not even with her irreversible and incurable condition as "woman (never married)," a census category now frozen into a kind of premature terminal illness. And she had kept her distance, contenting herself with whatever she got from Baldassare who (to tell the truth) never let her lack for anything. Now she was planning to reoccupy the place that she felt had been usurped for the past thirteen years: the house of her brother, inconsolably mourned. She didn't yet know, no one knew, that according to the will the house would be left to the other woman. Donna Adelina would discover this a month later, receiving as compensation the use of the small apartment and a few hectares of barren land, a civil case that proceeded for another eight years and an ulcer that would bring her an early death.

Not even Lucina Saccomanda knew. Perhaps that is why her eyes, as bright as her foreign seas, were nearly dry. Not because she wasn't grief-stricken. Not because she didn't owe something to the man who had plucked her out of a miserable existence, destined to marry a widower with five children in the best case or to prostitute herself around the port in the worst. Not because she hadn't loved that man, capable of sudden fits of rage, touchy and violent — but who, afterwards at night, shedding his jacket and pants, shaking off thoughts which she sensed were harsh and avaricious, dense with hatred and resentment, would melt inside her, so that violence and force were spontaneously transmuted into passion, liquid and hot. And despite knowing that all this was gone forever, Lucina's eyes remained dry, because she imagined that she would soon have to leave the house, in which she had felt like an unwanted guest for thirteen years, stung by Adelina's glances, judged by her silence and by the rare greetings bestowed not for her sake, but made obligatory by the fear that Baldassare Farrauto instilled, even when absent.

Lucina heard a shifting of chairs. Two more days of obligation and exhaustion still loomed, of hands shaken and grief displayed, burdens piled onto the pain she preferred to keep private. All she wanted was to throw herself in bed, in *their* bed, to put her face in the pillow and sleep, because dreams will revive the dead, and perhaps in the morning one can smile again.

Someone would leave, another would arrive. And the same old phrases would be repeated, condolences expressed almost with embarrassment, to stay on good terms with both women, not knowing who would end up with the bigger share, though with the mental reservation that custom and men's laws give precedence to ties imposed by birth over those chosen in life.

Lucina took pride in never having asked Baldassare to marry her, and the only time he — *he* — asked *her*, she answered him, laughing, "what you need is a nice girl." But Lucina had never lost sight of the fact that they'd been married ever since he'd spotted her at the port one evening and they had ended up making love under an overturned boat.

In the room with the coffin in the middle, the sister clinging like a barnacle to its dark wood, the chairs along the wall, and the motionless time of the pendulum clock, striking every quarter hour, the judge and his wife had spent the minimum twenty minutes necessary to properly render homage to the deceased and to his relatives and loved ones. Now they prepared to exchange salutations with the entire family pyramidically, from the sister downwards along all of its collateral branches. The judge bowed forward slightly each time he shook a hand, while with the other hand, hidden behind his back, he tugged on the dress of his wife, who tarried in making her last, long farewells.

Passing before the doorway to another room, the judge and his wife remained on the threshold, not quite knowing whether to limit themselves to greeting Lucina Saccomanda with a nod or to penetrate the circle of her solitude and shake her hand, since for some reason anything is permitted in the presence of the dead.

Their hesitation was short-lived. Lucina Saccomanda made the first move. She motioned the judge to approach. His wife remained in the doorway, in profile, one eye out for what was happening in the mourning chamber, the other alert and critical of the rudeness of beckoning her husband alone. Donna Adelina was right: shameless.

"Your Honor, please excuse me..."

"For heaven's sake, we were coming over anyway to express our condolences..." answered the judge, looking towards his wife for confirmation, realizing too late that she had stayed behind to stand guard.

"Thank you, Your Honor, and my thanks to your wife... but I need you for something related to the misfortune of my...of the..."

"Of our poor and eternally lamented mayor," hastened the judge in support of Lucina, who even dressed in the black of mourning revealed a shape and beauty unanimously — and never publicly — praised.

Lucina rewarded the judge with a smile for easing the awkwardness she felt, being unable to confer some respectable title on her relationship with the deceased — a resplendence of white teeth, which the judge gathered like a flower suddenly blossoming on those black clothes and black veils of grief.

"You see, Your Honor, two days ago I received a letter. One of those letters written by those who don't have the courage of their words..."

"I understand,..." said the judge, who got a bundle of them every week, with accusations and tip-offs on half the town, sometimes directed against himself, the king's judge, of impeccable virtue public and private. The judge imagined that Lucina must have received quite a few in those years of silent envy and anonymous insults.

"You see, Your Honor, I've always torn them up, because they're written by people of no importance. I've always believed that an insult is measured not by what it says, but by who says it. And if it's spoken by a nobody, then the insult does not exist."

"Exactly," said the judge, stunned by the syllogism, which he might have constructed by virtue of his classical and judicial studies, but surprising for a woman from who-knows-what harbor.

"But this letter is different," Lucina continued, drawing a sheet of paper from her sleeve. The judge took it delicately and read. A few lines, written in block letters:

GABRIELE TAIBBI WANTS TO KILL BALDASSARE FARRAUTO. HES' GOT A GUN ALREADY. WATCH OUT, IF YOU LOVE HIM. A FRIEND.

And the judge noted the misplaced apostrophe. "You showed this letter to your,..." he began.

"Yes, certainly. It just made him laugh. He said Taibbi didn't have the...well, that he didn't have the courage. But *someone* had the courage. They brought him home to me soaking wet. They left him out in the rain all night, there in the middle of the piazza..."

The judge bent over Lucina to alleviate the sobs that finally seized her. He put a hand on her shoulder, noticing its warmth. He also noticed his wife's irritated cough.

"Don't worry, I'll handle it. I'm going right to the carabinieri." And he turned to where his wife was waiting for him, the restless heel of her right shoe tapping the floor.

"Should we just stay here all night?" she whispered acidly.

"No, we're going, we're going," replied the judge. Before leaving he tried to see Lucina's shining eyes one more time.

But she held her head in her hands. She was crying in silence, alone.

6

It was starting to rain again. A soft rain. Thin. Some drops were caught by his green woolen jacket and winked feeble reflections of light before suffocating, absorbed by the cloth. The center of the piazza was empty — everyone had lined up along the walls, under the balconies, in the bars and shops that were still open, holding out against the dampness of that Tuesday evening.

Adano hurried along the walls, trying to avoid arms, legs, and looks. Behind him he heard footsteps and curses from Semino, who didn't even have the lieutenant's leather portfolio to cover his head. He noticed the looks of the silent men.

Semino caught him by an elbow. "*Tenente, lo hanno killed qui,*" he said, pointing to the dark smooth slabs of basalt pavement. *Lieutenant, this is where they killed him.*

Adano glanced fleetingly. No trace of the recent bloodshed. Last night's rain had washed it away. He didn't stop — he picked up his pace. It was raining harder now.

"It's raining," said a man's voice, muffled.

"Yeah," someone answered.

"Good weather, bad weather, no weather lasts forever," added another, putting an end to the conversation. Everyone knew these were days of folded arms, deserted fields, unemployed idleness only good for smoking and spitting on the ground.

Adano kept going. Semino was swearing. "Rain, rain and rain, *tuu mach*. How much does it rain in this town?"

The lieutenant took advantage of a wide, unoccupied sidewalk to hug the wall, in the dry protected rectangle under a balcony. He looked over his uniform — it was soaked.

Semino dried his forehead and hair with a white handkerchief. "San Biagio protect me from maladies of the throat, that's where I'm the weakest."

"Semino, why is it only us, here?"

"What did you mean, Lieutenant?"

"Why hasn't anyone taken shelter here, on this sidewalk?"

Semino looked around, stuck out his head and looked left and right. He smiled. "Ah, Lieutenant, this is the casino."

"Oh, I see..."

"No, what do you see? It's the gentleman's casino, the club. Look,..." and he pointed at the lights shining behind some French doors, at ground level a few meters down the street. "Here is where the people of the town meet, what do we call them in America? The misters, not the workers."

Workers. A memory came to Adano of his father, a vague memory of absence always justified by his work in the union, by a passion that Benjamin had never detected in their own rare encounters. Passion? More like a second-hand account of passion, reconstructed from the words of those who — to the jealousy and anger of the child — were able to spend time with that absent father. Yes, he should have been proud of his passionate father, a father who fought for the workers. So they said. A son's pride. The pride of a son orphaned in thought and in deed.

Hugging the wall, Adano neared the glass doors of the club. Across the street some peasants, hands in pockets, were following his movements with indifference. Looking in the salon, Adano made out an upright piano, a radio, and the feet of someone who appeared to have died in an armchair. He craned his neck. A man was sleeping, his head flung back, mouth open, the newspaper spread across his legs. There was no one else.

Adano slid along to the next French door, which opened onto the billiard room. Two men, resting their sticks on end, tall as lances, were observing a third stretched across the green felt, preparing to strike a ball. In a corner at the back were four more around a table, silent and still as they studied their cards.

Tableaux vivants. Living portraits. Or dead. *Nature morte.* Each French door framed a panel of motionless figures. Adano found himself smiling. He was thinking of the black and white of cinema, of the frames in a reel of film. He was thinking of the display windows of New York City department stores, of mannequins at night surprised by taxi headlights. And with a different smile he realized that he was twenty-six years old, that he would be leaving here soon, that the war would end and he would go home. He remembered that he was American, and he felt lucky. Not proud, but lucky.

"*...a hell-broth, boil and bubble...double, double, toil and trouble...fire burn, and cauldron bubble...*"

The pronunciation was half-chewed, uncertain, guessed-at. But Adano recognized the English. The voice came from the last of the four windows, ajar. He moved closer.

"*...double, double, toil and trouble...*"

"Macbeth," said Adano, even before looking inside the room.

The youth who was reading out loud heard him. He raised his eyes from the book and saw Adano. He was almost embarrassed at finding himself caught. He held up the book, giving a resigned nod in confirmation. He was smiling sadly, his eyes squinting from the smoke of the cigarette between his lips.

"Macbeth, the witches from Macbeth," said Adano. "*Double, double, toil and trouble. Fire burn, and cauldron bubble.*"

"I'll never be able to learn English this way. It works better with French," said the young man. "American?"

"Yes, but my father was born in Sicily, like my grandfather. He died though."

"You make dying sound like an accomplishment."

"At least in death we're released from our memory of others, from our grief, our tears. Death is awful that way — those who die continue to live in the memory and words of others."

The young man nodded, as though reflecting on those words. Adano remained standing outside the French doors, the other sitting in the armchair of what was perhaps a reading room.

"You don't speak Italian like an American, like a Sicilian from America..."

"I studied it. I studied Italian literature in New York."

"Ah, literature..."

"Dante, Petrarch, Pirandello."

"Then you're familiar with us, us Sicilians from around here. Too familiar, if you've read Pirandello..."

"A little. Some stories, the really beautiful one about the moon and the sulfur mine worker...what's it called?"

"Cìaula. 'Cìaula Discovers the Moon.'"

"Yeah, Cìaula. The name of a bird, I believe..."

"The crow, in dialect."

"Yeah,..." Adano was absorbed in thought. "You've studied literature too?"

The youth shook his head, extinguishing his cigarette, smiling. "No. I read. Whatever I can find, what there is to find around here. Not much. You have to go forty kilometers, at least as far as Caltanisetta, to find a book. And with a job..."

"You teach?"

"No, I'm employed by the farm cooperative. And you? As a civilian, I mean…"

"Nothing. I finished my studies, graduated just in time to get called up. First the Marines, now they've brought me to Italy, Naples…"

"Maybe they'll even send you to France, to Paris…"

"I'm hoping to go back home, really…"

"Paris," repeated the youth, lighting another Chesterfield. "The city of Voltaire. I'd like to go there some day. But here we are…." And he shrugged, skeptical and resigned.

"Here we are," echoed Adano.

"Here we are, a long way from everything. A long way from reason and from justice…but please, come in. I'm sorry, I didn't realize it was raining."

Adano looked for Semino and saw him greeting someone, acquaintances from his past as an invader of his own land in the train of Allied troops. Semino signaled not to worry. The lieutenant entered the room and dropped into a chair across from the youth. He sighed from tiredness and relief. The other one was observing him.

"Are you staying in town for long? Everyone in the club was talking about you tonight. You were the third topic of conversation, after the mayor's death. Not a bad spot, number three."

"And the second topic?"

"Women, as always."

"Women?"

"Women. Imagined, modelled in thin air, described, desired, insulted. Women for men whose only trace of a passage on this earth might be the depression left on the seat of an armchair in a club…armchairs like these."

"Including you?"

"Who knows, perhaps these times that seem dead and cold will be good for something." The young man enunciated these words in a strong Sicilian accent, with precision — a lucid precision, the mirror of a lively and restless intelligence. Adano tried to rouse him, to break through the veil of cigarette smoke that seemed to enclose him.

"You're young, you must be my age, more or less..."

"Twenty-three..."

"I was thinking more...you could go away, as soon as the war's over. You could move to the city, to Naples or Rome."

"Sometimes I get the impression that the world has shrunk to Sicily, this island, and within this island, the island of this town, and even deeper inside there's us, with our long-suffering anger, our resentment, our lives and our deaths. You'll go away and we'll stay here..."

"Before going away I'm supposed to finish my job. But I arrived late. I needed to talk to the mayor..."

"And you found him dead. I don't know what you were supposed to do, but even if you'd found him alive, you wouldn't have gotten much out of him. He was a man who spoke little, and even less about anything important..."

"Mind if I just ask you point-blank? In your opinion, who killed him?"

"Who knows. Maybe when they shot him, he was already dead in the hearts of his friends, as they say around here. And friends he had! The same friends who are now so enraged at his murderer..."

"Hundred-Ten."

"Yes..."

"Strange nickname..."

"They say it comes from a bet, a challenge thrown down by his grandfather, also a sulfur miner. He would eat a hundred and ten cactus pears, one after the other...I don't know if he managed to do it."

"That's not a few."

"No, it could even kill you. But the miners have no respect for death. They know that every day they go down the mine, a collapse or a methane leak could kill them. They live with death. They live in its belly. But maybe that nickname has another origin, less sensational and more concrete. Hundred-Ten's grandfather knew how to read and write, one of the few, and among his fellow workers he was like a professor, one in a hundred and ten, so to speak. These people believe in the written word, they believe that the pen is a sword that separates right from wrong. On the written word hangs their destiny, of salvation or damnation. Almost always damnation, for them..."

"And also for Hundred-Ten?"

"Look, I know the man. He's no doubt capable of theft, but not murder. But anyone could be mistaken, me or the judges. I daresay even a chief of the carabinieri could be mistaken."

Adano smiled at the shrewd irony. "I met him, the chief..."

"He's an idiot, but he understands right away what he's supposed to do. He didn't waste any time."

"You don't think it was Hundred-Ten. I don't either, from what little I know. I talked to his wife. I've seen his sons. Poor folks, desperate. And yet we can't do anything about it. We're paralyzed by this injustice that's happening right before our eyes."

"This is the injustice you're *seeing*, the one before your own eyes. And it makes you feel guilty. But it's only the latest, chronologically. That man, Hundred-Ten, was already living in injustice. The injustice of poverty and weakness, avenged by violence, by theft, by going in and out of jail until it becomes something to brag about. And their grandfathers and their grandfathers' fathers lived under the same injustice in a world far away from reason, and therefore, from justice."

"Sooner or later things will change. When the war's over..."

"The war's been over for some time, here. For many, it never happened. And you brought back those who'd been Fascists with flying colors. You brought back those who'd been mafiosi, asking for compensation. Some even got it. Yes, maybe things will change. I don't know if it'll be for the better."

"You're too pessimistic..."

"No, I was just born here."

The youth stubbed out his Chesterfield. Now they heard the sounds of billiard balls, of occasional voices raised in the furor of a card game.

"It's stopped raining," said Adano, looking outside. The church bell tolled nine times.

"It's late. Excuse me, I have to go home." The youth stood up, putting his book into his coat pocket. He shook the lieutenant's hand. Before stepping outside, he stopped to light another cigarette. The smoke from the Chesterfield made him squint. "...*dove siamo ora ci sono pugnali nei sorrisi degli uomini.*"

"*Where we are, there's daggers in men's smiles,*" Adano translated.

"*Macbeth. Ancora Macbeth. È strano che Shakespeare non sia nato in Sicilia,*" said the youth.

Macbeth, again. Funny that Shakespeare wasn't born in Sicily.

Night

1

Caracco did have a home, somewhere. But he felt hot. Maybe the wine, maybe his blood. There was a home, but he didn't remember where. Every night he tried to go there but got lost. The streets were too similar and too dark. He could never get further than the four steps of white stone in front of the Church of the Madonna of Itria. They appeared before him as he staggered out of the entrance of Pietro Giallonardo's wine shop. He peed in a corner of the piazza and saluted the deserted boulevard — a military salute, standing at attention. He'd been in the artillery in the Great War, on the Piave front. He collapsed on the steps, conquered by wine and heat.

The spot was sheltered from the wind and rain. Caracco slept, in the silence of the Corso Garibaldi. He was awakened by hurried steps. He opened his eyes. They were small, quick little steps. Like the steps of a woman. Aroused, Caracco tried to disperse the fog of the vinegary red wine he'd just been drinking. But there weren't any women, not at that hour, at night and in such damp weather. The steps came closer. Two short, fat legs passed before him as quickly as they could. Caracco rubbed his eyes, a useless attempt to restore lost clarity. He recognized the man who was running towards the piazza, forcing his two tiny legs. "An orange with feet," thought Caracco. He closed his eyes again, resting his head on the steps of the Church of the Madonna of Itria. But before going back to sleep, he was bothered by the vague sensation of having witnessed something unusual.

In fact it *was* unusual, given that those little legs belonged to Papandrè. Unusual, because never in living memory had he ever been discovered in the act, natural and spontaneous for many, of walking on his legs. Walking? *Running* even, on those little feet too miniscule for his enormously obese body, unaccustomed to transporting itself. But Papandrè *was* running, impelled by an urgency that made him push his weak legs, resulting in the profuse sweat that soaked his bare head in spite of the cold, damp evening.

Reaching one end of the piazza, he pulled a vast white handkerchief out of his pocket and wiped his forehead, neck, and throat. He was gasping. He started to run again, but his legs stopped following along. He was muttering a rosary of broken phrases.

"I'll make it, I'll make it...I won't make it...I'll make it...I won't make it."

He advanced to the center of the piazza. At the far end, next to the cathedral, he saw the light of his destination: the open door of the Mutual Aid Society, where every day the five-person card tables served as meeting places for the salesmen, artisans, and wealthy farmers of the town. Papandrè didn't frequent the Mutual Aid. He rarely left home, and never on foot. But an hour earlier the society's waiter had shown up to inform him of an urgent phone call.

"Fucking asshole, fucking asshole,..." Papandrè wheezily cursed Totò Asaro who, alerted, had not arrived in time with the car, forcing him to transport himself on foot. *On foot.*

The clock on the cathedral showed eleven o'clock. Papandrè feared that upon the first strike of the bell he'd be dead, since he'd never manage to reach the Mutual Aid in time to answer the phone call.

"I won't make it...I won't make it...I'll make it...I won't make it..."

The piazza became more elongated with each step. Out of the Mutual Aid Society came the waiter, astounded to recognize Papandrè emerging through the powdery mist of rain, bowling along down the middle of the square. "An orange with feet," thought the waiter. And, for the pleasure of straining the man's heart even further, he motioned Papandrè to hurry up.

Papandrè was flailing his arms, imploring through gestures: *wait, wait*. With one hand he wiped off his sweat, while the other arm windmilled wildly towards the Mutual Aid, towards the cathedral clock, to stop its hands, to stop time, to help himself swim through the air.

The sound of an engine. That's all he needed. Papandrè skidded to a halt, terrified of his own uncontrollable momentum, certain that in this accelerated world, he would end up under the wheels of the car.

Brakes. The automobile stopped next to Papandrè.

It was Totò Asaro. "I came to your house, but you'd already left. I'll take you...." He opened the door.

"Fucking asshole, fucking asshole," Papandrè cursed, and started running again.

Totò, at the wheel with the passenger door open, cruised alongside him. "Get in, for heaven's sake, can't you see you're soaked in sweat. You could get sick..."

Papandrè kept going, his breathing even more labored. "Fucking asshole, now you show up, now you show up, fucking asshole, now that I'm here, you'll take me, fucking asshole, fucking asshole, now that I'm here, I'll make it, I'll make it..."

And so he crossed the last seventy meters, step by step. Quick little steps, the black car beside him, open in an invitation indignantly refused.

All at once. The first toll of the church bell. The first ring of the telephone. Papandrè plunging into the Mutual Aid Society, leaning forward at a dead run as he flung wide its half-open door.

"Where is it, where's the phone, where is it?"

The waiter led him to the apparatus on the wall. Papandrè answered on the third ring. He leaned breathless against the wall.

"…"

He was gasping.

"…"

He wiped his head, his face, his neck.

"…"

He looked for a chair, but it was too far from the telephone.

"…"

He jerked upright.

"…I'm here…I'm fine….you must excuse me, I just ran… yes, ran, it's nothing to laugh about, my heart was about to burst…you were calling, I didn't want to make you wait… what, at midnight? It would be an honor…but why don't you come to my house?…I understand, that's right, out of caution, you never know…yes, I know it, the big farmhouse at Quattro Fanaiti…of course, I'll bring company…no problem…then I'll see you…my respects, Don Calò."

He hung up and stared at the phone, grimacing. "He laughs. What's there to laugh about? Two more steps and I would have departed this life. And he laughs."

He left the Mutual Aid partially restored. The waiter went back inside to turn off the lights and lock the doors. He had stayed late, but calls for Papandrè took absolute precedence.

Totò was leaning against the car. Smoking.

"You have to forgive me if I was late, Papandrè, but the car wouldn't start."

Papandrè approached. He waited for Totò to open the door.

"Fucking asshole, I could have died."

Totò Asaro bowed his head in an act of contrition, though inwardly pleased by this priceless, newly discovered Papandrè, hurtling across the piazza.

"An orange with feet," he thought, getting behind the wheel. And he started the car.

2

A cough. He opened his eyes. Pino was coughing again. He looked for him, he reached out a hand. His eyes adjusted to the light coming from the corridor through the spyhole in the iron door. Only then did Picipò realize that he was awakening in the cell where they'd stuck him the night before.

He closed his eyes. He opened them. In the darkness of the cell, only the rectangle of light from the spyhole. He'd slept. He'd done nothing but sleep. Asleep, he had answered the chief's questions — denying, denying, denying. That's all you can do in front of cops and judges. A conditioned reflex that kicked in despite the wine, the exhaustion, the humiliation, and the self-pity.

He'd been sleeping in the cell. An ominous, agitated sleep, slashed by the glint of a knife blade, soaked by the sweat of the mine, interrupted by Pino's coughing fits, visited by the uniforms of faceless carabinieri. And in his hand the cold metal of a pistol, in his ears the explosion of a shot, in his leaden legs an urge to run, behind his back the voices of men, on his face the breath of his wife and the pain of a wound, behind his eyes the darkness of night, in his mouth the desire for strong red wine.

"I'm thirsty."

No answer. The station was silent, as if deserted.

"I'm thirsty."

His own voice resounded within the cell and echoed through the chambers of the police station and returned without an answer.

He got up off his cot. He went to the slit in the door and shouted, "I'm thirsty."

Time stood still and silent until it was marred by the movement of a chair somewhere.

Steps, shuffling and slow. They stopped.

"I'm thirsty," shouted Vincenzo Picipò again.

"Calm down, I'm coming," replied the sleepy voice of Corporal Nanìa. He advanced a few more steps, appearing before the cell door. Picipò could make out his pale face shadowed by a veil of dark stubble, with rings under his eyes, the jacket of his uniform open to a tieless shirt.

"What do you want, Hundred-Ten?" asked Nanìa.

"I'm thirsty, Corporal. A little water."

"Aren't you sleepy?"

"Yes, but now I'm thirsty."

"All right."

The steps receded. Silence returned to the station. A gush of water. A sigh or maybe a yawn. More steps, closer. The door opened. Nanìa handed over a tin mug full of water. He waited for Picipò to finish drinking and hand back the cup.

"Thanks, Corporal. Is it raining?"

"I believe it's stopped."

"Nasty winter."

"Yeah, nasty."

"But what can we do, Corporal?"

"What do you want to do, Hundred-Ten?"

"It's just something people say."

"You really did it to yourself this time."

"They did it to me..."

"Forget that. You're better off talking, otherwise you'll be inside the rest of your life."

"What should I say?"

"The truth."

"Corporal, where are you from?"

"Salemi."

"You're Sicilian like me."

"So?"

"So, don't talk to me about truth. Whether I killed him or I didn't kill him, no one cares."

"You care. Think of your wife, your sons."

"I *am* thinking of them."

"And you're not thinking about what will happen to them without you?"

"Corporal, I'm thinking about my family. But someone wants to destroy me, someone who decided to get me into this mess. What do you think?"

"About what?"

"A hundred mouths are open."

"What do you mean?"

"Nothing, Corporal, nothing." Hundred-Ten lay down on the cot. The cell door closed. In the darkness, only the rectangle of the spy hole.

Corporal Nanìa returned to the front desk. He still had the empty mug in his hands.

"A hundred mouths are open," he repeated.

Now he felt better. His stomach had settled. The restored intestinal peace was even worth the chief giving him the night shift. Sergeant Di Dio was surely in some whore's bed — Nanìa heartily wished he'd contract some contagious disease of the kind that leads first to blindness and finally to dementia, severe enough to make death seem preferable. The chief, claiming profound exhaustion, had gone home to bed. And who had been left at the station? Corporal Nanìa, the rationale being that he had just returned from four days' leave, as if no one wanted to recognize how much he had suffered and endured due to an indigestion that, God forbid, could've had tragic, even mortal consequences.

"A hundred mouths are open," Nanìa reflected.

And he started to feel hungry. Having overcome his indigestion, he had digested the nausea as well. He opened the desk drawer and shoved aside papers, documents, and statements. At the bottom was a well-hidden, carefully wrapped package that his mother had given him before he left home. He set it on the middle of the table and unwrapped it with slow, calculated movements. Once open, he stuck his nose in it to enjoy the aroma. He picked up an olive between two fingers, the sweet black wrinkly kind. He turned it this way and that before his eyes, a tiny droplet of oil sliding down his thumb.

"*Bella*," he whispered to the olive, in a kiss of love.

He placed it delicately on his tongue, sucked on it, and thought of his mama. A tender drop of nostalgia welled in the corporal's right eye.

3

The English, deep down, are still Byronic. In the fourth chapter of the *Sicily Zone Handbook*, published in June 1943 by the Foreign Office, Adano re-read a sentence not devoid of literary influences:

> The head of the Palermo police has said that if a cross were to be placed on every spot where a victim lies buried in the plain of Palermo, the Conca d'Oro would appear as a vast cemetery.

That old passion for memorial columns and plaques, very English. And Adano recalled the few months spent in London before the war, with a girl from Brixton who dragged him to the cemeteries for kissing.

Outside it had almost stopped raining. Some pitter-patter still resounded off the roofs. The storm had immediately taken out the power lines — roads and houses were left in the dark. The owner of the hotel, supplying him with a kerosene lamp, reminded him of the blackout and recalled the nights before the landing.

"It was summer. We would go out into the fields, afraid of the bombs. All night we watched the sky, full of airplanes. Fires broke out all along the valley, from Agrigento to Canicattì. My wife's father is deaf, he didn't hear the roar of the planes, or the bombs. They seemed like fireworks to him, nothing dangerous or scary. He would open his umbrella and explain that nothing could harm him under there."

Adano had stayed in the lobby with the lamp. He wasn't sleepy, he wasn't ready to close himself up in a room that stank of dampness. He went back to reading the manual for Anglo-Saxon officers who required reassurance on the eve of their hostile landing in Sicily.

The anonymous editors had dedicated four columns to two words in italics, *Mafia* and *Omertà*. They cited Giuseppe Pitrè, a scholar of local traditions, sketching out a historical reconstruction of the phenomenon, dating it from the period when the Bourbons took refuge in Sicily, fleeing Napoleon. *For the English, it's always Bonaparte's fault.*

> The *Mafia* thus appeared as a loosely organised society under an unwritten code of laws, or rather ethics, known as *Omertà*. The most reliable etymology of this word is the word *Omu*, which, in vernacular, means a person who is conscious of his own rights; it is connected with the Italian *Uomo* and may roughly be interpreted as manliness.

Those romantic English. They write about virtue, of the awareness of the individual, of respecting one's rights, about self-made justice. Adano remembered the Mafiosi he knew from the streets of his neighborhood in New York, those Italian-Americans quick with a knife, wearing flashy suits with a pistol under the jacket, ready to smash your face or break your legs. The same ones who had forced Jerry Monreale's family to flee in the night, after they destroyed the display cases of their shop, set it on fire, and broke his father's arm. And one morning Benjamin Adano found the shop closed and his friend Jerry's house deserted. He heard the whispers of neighbors who — from behind closed doors — had listened to them leaving. He managed to enter the empty house. Among the furniture and possessions abandoned in the panicked flight, he found Jerry's new baseball glove and, shamefully, stuck it inside his jacket. Then he too made his getaway. Like a thief.

The hotel was silent. The silence slipped along the streets of the town. "Upon such a crime there follows silence," Adano read. "Were the murderer to be discovered he would suffer at the hands of justice the penalty of the law; but Mafia goes unpunished because no one will dare to denounce it, or, if one did, no one would bear witness against it."

He was struck again by the face of Hundred-Ten's wife, by the dark looks of his eldest son. Semino had gained Sergeant Di Dio's confidence: against Hundred-Ten there were not one, not two, but a whole army of witnesses. But what could Adano do? He'd be leaving the next day, leaving that town, never to return. And he would leave Hundred-Ten in his cell, leave his wife with her troubles, and his sons, probably, with their vendettas. And the list of injustices would still be counted off like beads on a rosary, undisturbed by Adano's accidental appearance, which hadn't changed anything, which couldn't change anything. He kept reading.

"Again, as a matter of Omertà, the innocent man charged with a crime will not utter a word to exculpate himself, and, if it so happens, takes in silence the penalty the law awards him, either as culprit or accomplice, while the guilty goes free and probably unsuspected."

It was already written, all of it. Everyone knew it. The Sicilians knew it and the English knew it, Adano knew it and even Hundred-Ten knew it. And his wife and his children knew it and whoever killed the mayor knew it and the chief and the young man who smoked Chesterfields and even the mayor knew it, before he was killed.

He needed air and stepped out of the hotel. The electricity was still out and might not come back that night. He breathed the dampness of the rain just fallen. He was alone, a dark shadow in the dark night, looking up at the starless sky.

First he heard the clatter of sheet metal and the rumble of engines. Then spears of light lit up the street. Two trucks, fast, passed by almost abreast, forcing him to the wall. Insignia erased, unit numbers painted over, plates unreadable, the tarpaulins ripped, but without any doubt the trucks Adano was looking for. The lieutenant ran to the middle of the street, until he could no longer make out the weak taillights. The noise of the engines still lingered, and then silence, again.

He stopped there, looking into the darkness.

He turned too late towards the screech of brakes, to the headlights that blinded him, to a curse he didn't quite catch. Not soon enough to get out of the way. His only thought was of dying. He shut his eyes.

Hearing Semino's voice, he opened them.

"Lieutenant, what are you doing in the *middle of the way*?"

Adano was still standing in front of the jeep's grill.

"Are you trying to kill yourself? Cause you're going to get killed like this," continued Semino, climbing anxiously out of the vehicle.

Adano nodded to Semino to reassure him. Fear had stripped him of speech. He realized that someone was sitting in the jeep. He looked closer, but the headlights kept him from recognizing who it was.

Semino noticed. "...A friend of mine...you know,..." he said under his breath.

Adano smiled. Semino was unruffled but contrite. Doubly contrite.

"They passed by here," Adano responded.

"*Who*?"

"The trucks, the stolen trucks. That's why I was in the middle of the street. I wanted to figure out where they were going."

Semino approached the lieutenant. He had to protect himself somehow, avoid a report that could make him lose everything. "Look, Lieutenant, do you really want to find those trucks?"

Adano studied Semino. "That's why we're here."

"I get it. Come with me." Then, turning to his friend, "Angelora, get in back, make room for the lieutenant."

"No need," said Adano, but the girl had already hopped into the back seat. It wasn't the first time she'd climbed into a jeep.

They flew down the nocturnal streets. Semino drove with assurance, unraveling the climbs and descents, the turns and alleys that disappeared into darkness. The girl put a hand on the lieutenant's shoulder and leaned into his ear. "Were you very afraid?"

Adano said no. He felt the girl's breath and the warmth of her hand on his shoulder.

"Get out, Angelora. You're home," was Semino's curt farewell.

They didn't wait for her to get inside. They left her standing there behind the jeep as it took off.

"Pretty," Adano commented.

"Yes, but she's a *whore*," said Semino, using the American word for it.

"Even I got that."

"Sorry, Lieutenant, I didn't mean to offend you."

"Not me, Semino, not me."

They fell silent. They passed through the dampness of the night, the fear within the darkened houses, the echoes of sleeping sighs, the bad dreams born of wine and poverty. The jeep stopped where the last dwellings of the town petered out into the countryside. Lights and voices filtered out between the planks of a wooden door. Semino knocked three times while Adano stood next to the vehicle. The door cracked opened. Semino muttered something to the man inside and invited Adano to follow him in.

The kerosene lamps weren't bright enough to reveal the faces of the men bent over a card table. Someone was carefully extracting cards from the deck, one at a time, accompanied by outbursts of cursing and arms raised to the heavens. Money was piled up on cards fanned out on the table.

"*Zicchinetta*," murmured Semino.

When they reached the circle of light, the game paused. They all turned to scrutinize Adano's uniform. The man who was dealing signaled them with a look: go back to playing your hands.

One of the players left the table and went up to them. Semino took his hand and tried to kiss it, but the man drew back with amused condescension. They stepped into a storeroom filled with stacks of burlap bags.

"Lieutenant, this is Father Gioacchino, the smartest man in this town."

"Let's not get carried away, Semino," the man shook his head.

"Father Gioacchino is a saint..."

"Don't listen to him, Lieutenant. He talks like that out of affection.... Of course, when you can do someone some good, in the name of the Lord..."

"Father Gioacchino, the lieutenant is here about that business we discussed..."

Benjamin Adano examined Father Gioacchino. He was heavily bundled up, and a gray scarf covered half his face. Only then did Adano realize that sticking out of his overcoat were the skirts of a monk's habit. Father Gioacchino sensed his astonishment.

"You're surprised to find me here, with these guys? Don't judge, Lieutenant. Christ reminds us we must open our arms to the prodigal son. I too am a lost lamb, and with these others I make my flock. I don't believe in these men of the cloth who sin in the sacristy and then punish from the altar. A sheep among the lost sheep, I stay with them, and what they lose at the card table serves the monastery and my brothers."

Adano realized that he was standing in the storeroom of a monastery. In the back, behind the sacks and staved-in barrels, was an enormous cross of dark wood covered in spiderwebs, old and forgotten.

"A saint, a saint," exclaimed Semino. Adano had never seen him so ecstatic, almost worshipful.

"Semino has spoken to me about your problem. What can I tell you? Lieutenant, those trucks used to be yours, but you would have taken them away, they would have been destroyed along the roads of Italy, you would have abandoned them in the field. But not here. Thanks to those trucks, workers are earning bread for their children. If they'd asked, you wouldn't have given them, so they were taken. Even the poor soldiers who were driving them, good and courageous boys like you, Lieutenant, got a small reward by doing a good deed, because this really is a good deed...even Hundred-Ten took one of those trucks, but then he behaved badly, he didn't respect the agreement — agreements have to be kept, right Lieutenant? — he didn't respect his obligations to the dear departed mayor...old squabbles, old history, but this has nothing to do with that mishap the other night...in any case, Lieutenant, forgive us our debts, as we forgive those of our debtors..."

"I saw those trucks tonight..."

"Of course you saw them, Lieutenant. We all see them, every day. You think a truck can be hidden just like this?" Father Gioacchino stuck a hand in his pocket and pulled out a walnut. "Now where did this come from?"

He cracked it between his strong fingers and extracted two pieces of the kernel, giving them to Semino and Adano. They received the white flesh in cupped hands, as if it was the host.

"Lieutenant, forget these trucks. Those who took them have paid or are paying. Like Hundred-Ten. Like the departed mayor."

"But they were stolen..."

"Don't use that word. One steals from those who don't want to give, but you came to help these people, to help us poor Sicilians, to help a community that opened its homes and offered you its friendship. Lieutenant, you can't rob someone who's trying to give you something..."

"Hear that, Lieutenant? A saint, a real saint," smiled Semino.

A violent curse reverberated from the roomful of card players. Father Gioacchino flinched as if receiving a blow. But with a smile on his lips.

"We curse Him, but maybe even this is a way to keep Him close." He lifted his eyes to heaven, to the ceiling of wood and mildew. "Forgive them Lord, they know not..."

4

She wiped the pearls of sweat off her thighs with the sheet, turned onto her belly, stretched her back, and stuck her head under the pillow. She was still breathing hard. She heard a match being struck and the whoosh of the flame as it devoured the sulfur tip, smelled the first puff of smoke from the cigarette lit by Barbaro. Saretta Taibbi might even be happy like this.

She felt cold. "Cover my shoulders..."

Barbaro pulled a corner of the blanket up to her neck.

Silence.

She could be happy like this. In that bed, in that house, in Barbaro's cigarette smoke, which burned her throat a little.

"I'll do anything for you," she abruptly declared. Barbaro was in profile, leaning against the headboard. A strong dark arm, a carpenter's, lay still on top of the covers. Saretta caressed it. "Anything."

"I know," responded Barbaro, drawing the last puff.

Silence.

"They could send him to prison," whispered Barbaro.

"It wasn't him. He's too much of a coward."

"He's your father."

"No, he's a pig. And he's worth no more than pig meat."

"He's still your father."

Saretta sat up. The covers slid down, revealing her large breasts, her thick nipples. "I did it for myself, but I also did it for you."

"I know, I know."

"And you? What did you do?"

"Me?"

"You were supposed to kill him like a pig, because you knew what he wanted from me. My father...and aren't I his daughter?"

Saretta stuck her head under the pillow.

Barbaro pulled the cover up to her neck. He stayed over her.

"I know..."

"You always say the same thing. *I know, I know*. But what do you know?"

"I know that...I mean...I know that you did it for us."

"No, I did it for me, because I didn't want him in this house anymore, looking at me that way...the pig."

"Saretta, don't be like this, I'm worried for you. If it gets out that it was you..."

"He knows it was me."

"He knows?"

Saretta sat up. She gazed at Barbaro with the eyes of a she-wolf. *This girl's crazy*, thought Barbaro.

"I told him myself, right after the mayor had that little talk with him."

"You told him about the letter?"

Saretta started laughing. "You should've seen his face. What a face. Dead. The face of a dead man. He'd started to cry in front of the mayor, he kneeled like he was praying to a saint..."

This girl is truly crazy — Barbaro was growing convinced.

"The mayor even gave him his pistol. 'Kill me. If you have the courage, kill me,' he said. 'Look me in the eye and shoot me.' The mayor was a real man, not a pig like him. And he was crying. He was acting like this: Excellency, I swear to you, on the soul of my dead wife, I never even thought about killing you."

Saretta's voice was shrill with crying and mean laughter, as she mocked her father's plea. "Mayor, why should I kill you? Who would want to harm a man of your generosity? I don't know anything, anything, I don't know anything. That letter was surely sent by someone who wants to hurt me, who wants to get me in trouble, some evil soul who wants to destroy me. Give me one day, Mayor, and I'll find out everything for you. One day and we'll fix everything, I swear to you on my wife, who sleeps in the bosom of the Lord..."

She's completely crazy. Barbaro was now sure of it.

Saretta was waving her arms now, half naked. "And he came home sick with fear. I felt sorry for him, you have to feel sorry for a sick pig. So I told him I was the one who sent the letter, because I'd heard his conversation with Totò Asaro and Mommino Falletta. I'd heard them ask him to hide the gun, to keep it at home until the day when they were supposed to kill the mayor. Because he didn't have the courage to kill him. Someone else does the hard part. He's too spineless to kill. The pig looked at me and said nothing. He was afraid even of me."

"And when he told the mayor it was you who wrote the letter?"

Saretta shook her long hair until it covered her eyes.

"He couldn't. They killed the mayor while the pig was still looking for him. And then he ran away."

"What if he comes back?"

"If he comes back, they'll arrest him. And if they don't get him, I'll kill him myself. With him gone, it's just you and me. Whenever we want, as much as we want."

Barbaro was silent now before this demoness.

Saretta fell back. She lifted the blanket that half-covered her. She spread her legs.

"Take me. Again."

This girl is too crazy, was Barbaro's final thought before plunging into her.

5

The man couldn't sleep. More than the fear, it was the pain in his joints that gave him no rest. And then the night: he wasn't used to the noises, the whistles and clicks of the dark countryside, the slow dripping of rain, no longer coming from the sky but from the olive branches, from the almond trees, from the leafless grapevines that stretched out their claws of twigs and shadows.

The dampness of a night in the open was new to Gabriele Taibbi, despite the fact that his official prison record listed his trade, along with an endless list of prior offenses, as that of a farm laborer. But in his forty-seven years, he had amassed perhaps thirty-two days of laboring. He had certainly never slept in the countryside after sunset. He was intimidated by the darkness, the leering white glances of chalky rocks in the moonlight, the sinister swaying of trees, the gloomy or strident cries of the beasts who inhabited the empty silence of nighttime. And this was one fine autumn night, cold and wet from recent rains.

"But who made me come here?" he thought, pulling the blanket up to his eyes, again. But he knew. He'd made himself do it, out of fear. Fear they would come to get him. The carabinieri at his door or maybe the others, his friends.

He was going mad. Still confused, he thought back to the piss he was halfway through taking just the night before, facing a wall on the corner behind the Church of Sant'Anna. Over his shoulder he'd heard two men walk quickly past, talking about the murdered mayor and how the cops were looking for whoever shot him and how long the guy had before he ended up in jail. Gabriele Taibbi had wet his pants in the shock that made him lose control of the arc and direction of his stream as he unleashed an obscenity against his daughter, the cause of his ruin. "Saretta, that lying bitch!"

He remembered coming up to the high stone ramparts of the abandoned castle. Castle? Four old walls and blocks of white stone tumbling onto the neglected grounds. That's all he needed, a castle, home to bats from half the province. But he didn't know where to go, and the street itself and his feet and the sight of the castle glowering over the town from on high had brought Gabriele Taibbi straight to it. Just for tonight, so tomorrow he could find someplace better, drier at least...

"Who is it?"

His skin clenched. A shadow — no, a noise — like a step, like an animal, maybe a man, maybe worse, souls condemned to the inferno, souls in purgatory, pray for me, O Lord my Lord, save me, by the Father and the Son and the Holy Spirit. He listened to his own breathing.

High above, from on top of the wall, a sound almost like metal against stone, like a rusty chain, a broken hinge, an empty can.

"Is someone there?" he whispered this time. Just to find his voice, to give himself the courage he'd never had, least of all tonight.

There was no one. No one. Maybe it was better that way. Or worse. He pulled the blanket over his head. In the dark warmth of the wool, stinking of dampness, he counted the labored beats of his heart.

He didn't have time to comprehend.

Who was grabbing him. Who was squeezing his throat. Who'd got on top of him. Who was throwing punches at his head.

He fainted from terror.

...

"Gabriele, are you still breathing?"

A voice.

"Gabriele, do you hear me?"

Father Son and Holy Spirit, I am dead, Father Son and Holy Spirit, forgive me for my sins, blessed souls of purgatory, welcome me among you, Holy Mary, Mother of God, don't leave me in limbo, Father Son and Holy Spirit...

"Gabriele!"

"Yes, Lord, I'm ready..."

"Gabriele, what are you talking about?"

He opened his eyes. He was stretched out on the ground. He opened his eyes and discovered that God was Don Calò and Saint Peter was Papandrè and the angels of the hereafter had the same faces as the fellow miscreants of his entire earthly life, the faces of Totò Asaro, of Mommino Falletta, of Sasà Bellavia, of Nino Montana Lampo, of Tanino Grisafi — who everyone called Bedwetter — of Gerlando Ciotta Bartolotta, of Nene Catalanotte — who everyone called Little Onion — of Big Pietro and Little Pietro, of Santino Lattuca. And what were they all doing in heaven? Hell, that's what this was.

"Gabriele, get up," ordered Don Calò.

Taibbi managed to get to his feet. He touched his sore temples. It was dark, wherever it was. A lantern shone feebly. It seemed to be an olive oil factory, at least judging by the bitter smell of fresh oil.

Again he examined Don Calò and Papandrè and the other angels of this damp, fearful night. He reluctantly concluded that he was alive, at least for the moment.

"Don Calò, forgive me."

"Why, Gabriele? Have you done something wrong?" The voice was soothing, a threat.

"I have many sins."

"I'm not your confessor, Gabriele. You know what your only sin is?"

Taibbi did not know.

"Your sin is that of being a fuck-up and of having a lying bitch for a daughter, speaking with respect."

"That's true, Don Calò. I was thinking the same thing."

"That's what everyone thinks." Don Calò pointed to the circle of men with Taibbi at its center. The gesture granted them permission to smile. Even Papandrè smiled, with an odd gurgle in his bull neck.

"You know you've gotten yourself in trouble?"

"Yes, Don Calò. I'm doomed."

"You ran away. But where did you think you were going?"

"I don't know, I swear I don't know."

"So why didn't you go to your friends?"

"I don't know."

"Who's rich in friends is poor in troubles. You know this, right?"

"I know."

"But your friends found you right away. You know why?"

"I don't know."

"Because you're a fuck-up. You know?"

"Yes."

"Because only fuck-ups hide in the castle, the first place they think of. The cops were also about to show up there..."

"The carabinieri?"

"Yes, Gabriele. Because they're lesser fuck-ups than you."

"Help me, Don Calò."

"That's why we're here. Come over here, Gabriele."

Taibbi approached.

"Bend down a little, Gabriele."

He bowed in guilty fear, like a child expecting a slap.

Don Calò grasped an ear between his fingers and twisted it.

"That hurts, Don Calò."

"I know it hurts."

"*Ow*, Don Calò, you'll tear it off."

"I won't tear it off, because with this ear you need to hear what I'm telling you. Do you hear me?"

"Yes, *ow*, Don Calò, I hear you good."

"Bravo. You know what you have to do tomorrow?"

"No, *ow*, I don't know, *ow*..."

"You're going to the cops."

"At the station?"

"Bravo. And you know what you're going to say?"

"No, *ow*, I don't know."

"You'll tell them everything. You'll tell them you're a fuck-up and that your daughter is a lying bitch who lets Barbaro fuck her, and she wanted to have you arrested by the mayor because you're a fuck-up, and you wanted to fuck your own daughter. Do you hear me alright?"

"Yes Don Calò, *ow*, you're hurting me."

Don Calò relaxed his hold. Gabriele Taibbi's ear was glowing red.

"Listen closely, Gabriele. Gerlando, come here."

Gerlando Ciotta Bartolotta stepped forward from the ranks of angels. He had the face of a good kid — alert eyes, handy with a gun — and a clean record, since no one had ever accused him of the two homicides he had committed on Don Calò's behalf, requested through Papandrè.

"Gerlando, tell Gabriele what happened three days ago," said Don Calò.

Gerlando Ciotta Bartolotta, as if on stage, began to recite a statement all ready to be typed, signed, and witnessed.

"On Sunday afternoon, the mayor Baldassare Farrauto approached me on the street and informed me that he had received an anonymous letter from an unknown person warning him that there was a certain Gabriele Taibbi with ill intentions regarding the mayor himself..."

"Bravo, Gerlando, continue," prompted Don Calò.

"He had me read the letter, or rather he read it to me himself, and I urged him not to be afraid. A short time later — it was already getting dark — we saw Taibbi in front of the cathedral. The mayor turned away from me and went to take Taibbi by the arm, and the three of us proceeded towards the soccer field."

"Gabriele, are you paying attention?"

"Yes, Don Calò."

"Bravo. Go on, Gerlando."

"On arriving there, the mayor showed the letter to Taibbi, confronted him with its contents, and asked him, 'Are you the one who's supposed to kill me?' Then I pulled my pistol out of my pocket and as a challenge I offered it to Taibbi, to whom I said, 'Take it, shoot him.' But Taibbi declared himself innocent and said he didn't know anything. Actually, while saying he didn't know anything, he promised at the same time to make an urgent effort to determine the letter's author, someone who presumably wished him harm. After that discussion, he promised us that within a day he would find out something about the person who had written the letter. Among other things, he told the mayor that there was a dangerous individual who wished him harm, but didn't name him."

"Bravo, Gerlando."

Gerlando Ciotta Bartolotta rejoined the choir of angels, his friends and colleagues.

"So, what do you need to do now, Gabriele?" Don Calò pressed.

"I don't know..."

"Then you are truly a fuck-up. Come over here..."

"No, Don Calò, I get it. Tomorrow I go to the carabinieri and tell them what happened…"

"Bravo. Name Gerlando as a witness."

"I'll name Gerlando as a witness…"

"Confess to the carabinieri that your daughter is a lying bitch and that she wrote the letter because you were threatening to kill her lover…"

"But how does that make me look…"

"It makes you look like the fuck-up and asshole you are. And you should be grateful for that. Then you explain that just last night, while you were looking for the mayor to clear up the matter, you found out that they had killed him…"

"But…"

"Shut up. Out of fear, you ran off."

"That's true."

"It's true because you're a gutless asshole. But you have witnesses, right here, Sarino Lattuca and Tanino Grisafi, able to confirm that at the moment of the crime, you were having dinner with them. And then?"

"Then what, Don Calò?"

"Did you get what Gerlando said? Did you hear that you told the mayor that someone wanted to cause you harm?"

"Yes, I heard."

"Who is this person you didn't name?"

"I don't know."

"But you do know, asshole. It's Vincenzo Picipò, called Hundred-Ten, a dangerous individual who wanted to hurt you. Why? Because he'd confided in you about wanting to kill the mayor and had asked you to help him, but you didn't agree and even threatened to expose his plan. Get it?"

"Now I get it, Don Calò,"

"Good, but a fuck-up you'll always be."

"I know."

6

There were shadows. There were flames and torches. There were dark caves. There were horses' hooves. There were shouts in the night. There were policemen's footsteps. There were black hoods. There were dark eyes. There were dreams.

He knew he was dreaming. He heard, even dreaming, Pino's coughing and the fitful sobbing of his mother. He knew he was dreaming. He wanted to dream. And he dreamed with the words of Ciccio Alaimo Di Loro, the carpenter who came around telling stories of the Sacred Avengers of St. Paul, of Coriolanus of Floresta, of Friar Diego La Matina. He dreamed the sound of the words, the unhurried tone, the nasal pronunciation, even the lengthy pauses of Ciccio Alaimo Di Loro. And in the dream he knew he was dreaming, he astonished himself by remembering entire passages of the tale, but then convinced himself — still in the dream — that the memory was Ciccio Alaimo Di Loro's. When anyone asked him why he never forgot anything, he'd say he had a secret, tapping the middle of his forehead.

And he dreamed he was blindfolded, Blasco di Castiglione or Angelo Picipò, who now in the dream were the same, but he was the only living man among puppets and figures like those painted on the sides of the carts and on the curtains of the storytellers who came to town in September before the harvest. And he dreamed he was in a twisting underground passage, being led by the hand, feeling the air turn cooler and then made warmer by the breath of the men assembled there. He heard a voice: "Blasco di Castiglione, you find yourself before the tribunal of the Sacred Avengers of St. Paul..."

And he was — as he dreamed — in a cavern, in the center of which stood an altar with a crucifix, illuminated by the torches hanging on the walls, in niches carved out of the rock. Around him were masked figures in penitents' robes, with daggers in their belts. The one who spoke, by his mien and manner of dress, appeared to be the head of that shadowy sect of administrators of justice. And Blasco, who was Angelo, rose to his feet, and twenty hands from which protruded twenty sharpened blades were pointed at his chest. The leader commanded, "Lower your daggers. Don Blasco will harm no one unless they interfere with our justice."

And he saw himself laughing, disdainful of any peril, impudent in his courage. And the leader of the sect spoke with the voice of Ciccio Alaimo Di Loro and moved his hands like the puppets of Tano Bammino. "You are young, Don Blasco, inexperienced in many things. You believe we are unjust in our love of justice. What is a man before a violated right? What is a human life before justice, which follows its own path? Pity those who get in its way — they will be crushed. Hear me, good sir..."

He remained silent, Blasco di Castiglione or Angelo Picipò, dreaming though aware of his brother Pino's coughing and the sobs from his mother's bed. He was silent, yet he questioned the leader of the sect, who replied thus, with firmness and pride: "We stay hidden because the shadows are necessary for our work. They are our strength and our security. The king's justice is administered by men who view it not as a duty, but as a salary. Their job is not to recognize the rights of each man, but to uphold the strong over the weakest. The strong are the landowners, the state officials, the lords, the clerics. These have rights that do not belong to the others, the weak. A knight who kills finds tolerance. A peasant who commits the same crime dies on the gallows. A noble can strip everything away from his vassal, and this is a right. This same right sends the vassal to the gallows for stealing some grain or a lamb from his master. And this is called justice..."

In the dream, Don Blasco di Castiglione spied his father, Vincenzo Picipò, in a corner of the cave of the Sacred Avengers of St. Paul, wearing trousers over his woolen underwear because he had to follow the chief of the carabinieri. And the leader of the sect, with a wave of an arm pulled by strings, pointed out Vincenzo Picipò to Don Blasco, who didn't recognize his father because he was Blasco di Castiglione, but he knew that the man with trousers pulled over his woolen underwear was the father of Angelo Picipò. And the voice of Ciccio Alaimo Di Loro, also now in the cavern of the Sacred Avengers of St. Paul, went on. "We must impose true justice and we have but one weapon: terror. And we have but one means of delivering it: mystery, shadow. We do not stay hidden out of cowardice, but out of necessity. We defend the weak and the poor!"

Ciccio Alaimo Di Loro fell silent. And everyone watched him, waiting. Don Blasco di Castiglione waited. He waited for the leader of the sect, the threads drooping from his arms. And beside the leader, hanging from the roof of the cave on metal hooks, their threads slack, the other puppets in black cloaks waited. Ciccio Alaimo Di Loro pressed a finger to the middle of his forehead as though he wanted to pierce it. He seemed to be saying, "I don't remember, I don't remember." But he was laughing. He always said that to provoke an outcry from the children begging him to finish the story, until he would turn his finger on his forehead, like a key in a lock, and the memory came back.

And Blasco di Castiglione heard a cough from his brother Pino and a sigh from his sleeping mother. He opened his eyes and became Angelo Picipò again, but he didn't find the black cloaks, the Sacred Avengers of St. Paul, the dagger blades, the burning torches. And he didn't find his father, taken by the carabinieri to the station in trousers pulled over his long woolen underwear.

DAY

1

"*Mericano.*"

At first, he didn't understand the word, but he caught the sound of it.

"*Mericano, a te dico.*" *American, I'm talking to you.*

Under the arch of ancient stone it was dark and stank of sewage.

"Over here," said the voice.

The stench provided further confirmation for Adano — the voice was coming from the latrine. He read the faded sign: "*Cessi pubblici.*" *Public toilets.*

"*Dice a me?*" asked Adano.

"Aren't you American?" replied the voice.

Adano approached the latrine. The man had a gaunt face, eyes swollen with fever. His oversized trousers, held up by a string, ballooned around his legs, exposing two thin bare ankles in old leather shoes.

"Got a cigarette?"

"Sorry, I don't smoke."

"Then you got fifty cents?"

Adano pulled a dime out of his pocket and held it out. But the man grasped his wrist and pulled it towards him, into the shadow and stink of the latrine.

"*Mericano,* don't be afraid. Do no evil, fear no evil. Have you done something evil?" The man was in the lieutenant's face, tightly squeezing his wrist to keep him from getting away. His eyelids were red and swollen from conjunctivitis.

"*Mericano,* you know how to read?"

The lieutenant nodded confusedly.

"Then read." The man raised his black cloth beret, showing off a hairless cranium. "I have a newspaper in my head, you know how to read?"

Not knowing what to do, Adano acknowledged the surreal comedy, though hastily pulling away from the lunatic's hands and from the oppressive stench of ammonia and stagnant piss.

"You're a soldier...what kind of soldier are you?"

"Marine..."

"*Marina*? A navy man! Not a soldier of the trenches? Mountain fighter, signal corps, engineer, artillery..."

Adano was in no mood to educate a stinking, drunk Sicilian on the branches of the U.S. Armed Forces. "No, a Marine," he repeated.

"You're wrong, soldier. The *navy* wasn't on the Piave front. The artillery was there. The gunner Sebastiano Caracco, son of Giovanni and Rosa, born 1895, called up the 15th of November 1915, Third Artillery, was present..."

"Good, I have to go..."

"Don't you want to talk with a soldier of the Great War? You know about war, *Mericano*? Have you fought a war, soldier of the navy? I've never seen you. In war you die. And you're alive, so you haven't fought a war. The gunner Sebastiano Caracco was dead once, on Hill 132. There was snow, soldier. Is there snow in Merica? You've seen it? Caracco's seen it. White as ice. *Cold* as ice. Under the snow you get warm and sleepy. And under the snow you die.... His comrades were calling: Sebastiano, Sebastiano, we have to leave. But Sebastiano Caracco died, on January 3rd 1917..."

"I'm sorry..."

"You think I've gone mad, soldier? No, I'm not mad. I'm dead. The dead are like the mad. They see everything, they know everything, they say everything because no one listens to them. Quiet, soldier. A windmill advances towards me, I run, and it pursues me…"

"Bravo…"

Caracco yanked the lieutenant's arm violently.

"Don't treat me this way, Mericano. Show respect to the soldiers, the valiant dead soldiers of the Third Artillery…"

Adano managed to break loose.

"You're leaving, soldier? You got a cigarette?"

"I don't smoke…"

"The other night, I was dead, because I died on Hill 132, and — being dead — I was going home, Mericano, and I was passing the old tower…you know where the old tower is, near the cathedral?"

The lieutenant continued his retreat to evade Caracco's foul breath, stinking of wine and rotten teeth.

"You know Hundred-Ten, soldier?"

Adano stopped.

"You have to listen to me. The newspaper's here in my head, but the words don't cooperate. I know Hundred-Ten. A shared glass of wine, a sardine, a boiled potato. We were in the mine, Mericano, pick-axe boys we were, but now I'm out of work. Got half a buck?"

"Here."

"Bravo, Mericano. You're a good man. Thank you."

Caracco pocketed the change. They were under the stone arch. More filthy water was draining from the latrine.

"The other night — when I was dead — I saw Hundred-Ten by the old tower. He was running, and I called him, I shouted, 'Hundred-Ten, Hundred-Ten.' But he didn't hear me, he was moving fast towards the piazza. So I got reminded that I really was dead, because he didn't turn around. Then Hundred-Ten stopped, but without seeing me. And there was a shot, a gunshot, and Hundred-Ten turned around, he went down Baronessa Street, you know Baronessa Street, there under the old tower?"

Caracco had stuck his hands in his pockets and was moving his trousers up and down, rocking back and forth in time.

"Mericano, did you know the mayor? They killed him. Are you sorry? They killed me too, on Hill 132, but no one's sorry."

2

"Sit down, Picipò."

Hundred-Ten advanced slowly, shuffling his feet like you do when you're beltless, holding up your pants.

He reached the chair. The chief had his nose in some papers. Corporal Nanìa, behind Hundred-Ten, sat at the typewriter, resting his chin on his hand. Sergeant Di Dio stood by the window, smoking and studying the sky.

"It's going to rain some more," he said. No one answered.

Hundred-Ten wiped his sweaty hands on his trousers. Silence.

Chief Perez moved away from the desk, still reading. He brushed past Hundred-Ten, who noticed his fat man's smell and then heard the murmur of his conference with Nanìa, though he couldn't quite make out the words. Sergeant Di Dio searched the sky for something only he knew about.

"Picipò, Vincenzo...." The chief's voice was now right behind him.

Hundred-Ten didn't turn around.

"Picipò, Vincenzo...." Perez used the same tone to repeat the same words.

He didn't answer.

"Listen to me, Picipò. You've got one chance. And I'm telling you against my own interest as commander of this station. For the crime you've committed, you deserve the penitentiary...and you've got a record. But as a man..."

"Speaking man to man..." the sergeant commented almost to himself, continuing to examine the sky.

"As a man, as the head of a family, Picipò," resumed Perez, slightly irritated, "the head of a family like you, I feel a duty to advise you that if you admit everything, if you explain that you acted in the grip of wine and anger, surely that would be taken into consideration, your situation might be treated, as they say, with leniency..."

"Confess," the sergeant urged him dully, putting out his cigarette under his shoe.

"Sergeant, you're turning this room into a pigsty, speaking with respect...." Perez responded irritably.

"There aren't any ashtrays, Chief," Di Dio defended himself.

"Toss them out the window. And leave it open, it's so smoky..."

"At your command, Chief." And the sergeant picked up the butt between two fingers, opened the window, and tossed out the remains of the cigarette.

"Well, Picipò?"

Hundred-Ten hunched his shoulders pointedly.

"I understand...." The chief passed by him again, holding his chin in a reflective pose. "I understand." He dropped back into his chair. He put his arms out on the desk, keeping his head down. Slowly, studying the effect, he lifted his gaze towards Picipò.

"Hundred-Ten, we questioned your wife again..."

Picipò didn't answer. He didn't trust the chief.

"She told us everything, Picipò. Everything. It's over, Picipò. In two hours you'll be in the prison at San Vito..."

"And you'll never get out," added the sergeant.

The chief, hopelessly resigned to the sergeant's annoying, pigheaded horseshit, proceeded imperturbed.

"Picipò, think of your children..."

Hundred-Ten, motionless, felt his eyes burning. He prayed not to be exposed by a tear.

"I understand. Corporal, read Maria Merulla Picipò's statement."

Nanìa cleared his throat. "Territorial District of the Royal Carabinieri of..."

"Skip ahead, Corporal, we know this,..." Perez urged him on, impatiently.

"Yes, then...Official Report of the Interview of Maria Picipò, née Merulla, of..."

"Not necessary, Corporal, Picipò knows when and where his wife was born. Let's get to the point for God's sake."

"At your orders, Chief. Then...before the undersigned officers of the judicial police here present is the aforementioned Maria Merulla Picipò, who, duly questioned, declares..."

"Finally..."

"...duly questioned, declares: on the evening of the sixth last, my husband came home shortly after the Ave Maria. He had a contusion on his right cheek. Upon my questioning, he spoke of having sustained it in a fall. There were at that moment two neighbors present in my home...is this good, Chief?"

"Yes, Nanìa, excellent. Continue."

"My husband having expressed his desire to go to bed and having begun to take off his shoes, my neighbors departed. After a few minutes had passed, my husband, changing his mind, told me that he had to go to the piazza and would return immediately."

"Is that so, Picipò?" asked the chief, staring at Hundred-Ten. But he got no answer. "Read, Corporal."

"So saying, my husband got up and approaching the dresser, opened the drawer, took out something I didn't see, closed it, and left."

"So, you didn't stay in bed, Picipò?"

Hundred-Ten wasn't even listening. He was fighting the urge to cry.

"Go on, Corporal."

"At your command, Chief. Seeing the confusion of which my husband..."

"That's 'contusion', Corporal, con-*too*-zhun, got it?"

"Of course, Chief. Seeing the contusion of which my husband bore obvious signs, I became suspicious that said injury had not been caused by a fall, and so deducing what his intentions might be, I placed myself in the doorway in the hopes of stopping him. I shouted, "Stop, for God's sake, do you want to destroy us?" But my husband pushed me violently aside and left, followed by me still shouting after him, hoping to bring him back, "You'll destroy us, you'll destroy us.""

"Picipò...your wife was right..."

Hundred-Ten, looking down, was inspecting his shoes.

"Read the rest, Nanìa."

"As my efforts were in vain, I knocked on the door of my mother, who lives four houses down from me, in the hopes of gaining her help, but without waiting for a response, I continued in pursuit of my husband, which was also in vain. Therefore, I returned home. Along the way, as I was about to reach my destination, I heard a gunshot coming from the piazza..."

"You shot the mayor...isn't that so?"

Vincenzo Picipò remained frozen.

"Entering my home," continued the corporal, "I awaited my husband, who returned after about ten minutes. I reprimanded him for going out and refusing to listen to me. He responded, 'I'm here now. Make the bed so I can go to sleep.' Soon after my son Angelo also came home."

The chief went and stood beside Hundred-Ten, bending over him.

"Well, Picipò?" he whispered in his ear.

"My wife doesn't talk like that," said Hundred-Ten, barely breathing.

"Well Picipò?" the chief said again.

Hundred-Ten swallowed in silence.

"I see." Perez moved towards his desk. "Nanìa, take him back to the holding cell."

Hundred-Ten, still holding up his trousers, went towards the door that Nanìa had already opened. Before leaving, he said in a firm voice, "Chief, it wasn't me who killed him. And that is what I'm truly sorry for."

Perhaps a tear was trembling on Hundred-Ten's cheek. Chief Perez was stunned. But he spread his arms in a shrug, thus negating any private shock, any doubt or qualm, and above all that insufferable tear.

3

"Totò, go open the door."

Totò Asaro obeyed. Papandrè was eating ricotta with sugar and bread by the spoonful, his gluttonous baby eyes narrowed to slits.

He concentrated on the sounds reaching him there, inside. From the voice, he deduced the identity of the man at the door.

"Show him in, Totò," he shouted in the direction of the entrance.

Beret in hand, Gabriele Taibbi appeared in the doorway of the room, followed by Totò.

"Sit down, Gabriele. You want some?" Papandrè pointed to the sugared ricotta.

"Thank you, no."

"So?"

"So, I'm here."

"You went to the police station?"

"Of course."

"You explained everything?"

"Just like we discussed."

"And this is good. Problems?"

"None, Papandrè. After three hours I was dismissed from the station."

"And this is good."

"Then I came here."

"Why?"

"To let you know."

"But I never doubted, Gabriele."

"So you can tell Don Calò not to worry."

"Don Calò isn't worried, Gabriele. Do I look worried to you?"

"No, Papandrè."

"Exactly. I'm calm. Clear skies fear not the thunder. You know that, right?"

"Sure..."

"So?"

"I did my duty."

"And that's what you were supposed to do. Your duty."

"So, I'm not worried?"

"Gabriele, you mustn't worry, you know why?"

"No..."

"Because your friends aren't worried, and they love you. See?"

"Completely, Papandrè."

"And this is good."

"So I can go home then?"

"To your daughter?"

"To my daughter. The police chief talked to her, too... she confirmed it."

"Bravo."

"So I'm going?"

"Go on, Gabriele. Totò, go with him."

Papandrè's eyes followed Gabriele through the door. On his return, Totò wore his usual vacant expression.

"Can we be sure?" asked Papandrè.

"The only sure thing is death."

"You always exaggerate, Totò."

"It's just a saying, Papandrè."

"Sayings are how you say what you really mean."

"I'm lost, Papandrè."

"Because you don't listen to me..."

"You're too smart for me."

"And you're too much of an ass-kisser for me."

"But...I didn't mean to offend..."

"Never mind, Totò. How does Gabriele seem to you?"

"He's got the runs."

"He's got the runs, like you say."

"He can't hold anything in."

"Very true, Totò. And so?"

"Can I tell you what I think?"

"Of course, Totò, you're like a son to me."

"He doesn't make it to Christmas."

"Totò, Christmas is a holy day. When Our Savior was born. After Christmas, Totò, after Christmas we'll handle it."

"Just say the word."

"Don't worry yourself about it, Totò. It's bad for the blood. You want some ricotta with sugar?"

"No thanks, my tooth hurts."

"Then get it pulled. I'm always telling you. You suffer once, then you never have to think about it again."

"That's true."

"Of course it is. But you never listen to me, Totò."

4

Clutching the package of broccoli, dry beans, and three artichokes to his chest, the judge proceeded quickly on his way, looking neither right nor left, avoiding the people assembled in the middle of the piazza.

Crossing the threshold of the club, consigning the broccoli, beans, and artichokes to the waiter, he was finally safe, like a ship riding out a stormy night in the harbor. But the noises of the piazza reached into the club — the voices of the men gathered around a pair of red flags in the cold morning wind, asking for land and work.

The judge entered the salon. Ignazio Mulè, the lawyer Giangreco, and Professor Brucculeri were by the windows, hands in pockets, a disgusted smirk on their faces. The judge slid down into an armchair and immersed himself in *The Daily Sicilian*.

"Bums," commented Mulè.

"Poor guys, asking for work," replied Brucculeri, who at certain times of year, particularly in autumn, betrayed feeble insurrectionist tendencies, the cold ashes of a youth spent as a Fascist revolutionary and admirer of D'Annunzio.

"Don't get me started, Professor. They're just bums."

"Actually, they're communists."

"No, Professor, you're not following me. These guys don't want to work. That's all," insisted Mulè.

"It's been raining for a week. There's no work for anyone."

"Professor, have you turned into a Communist by any chance?"

"For pity's sake."

"Watch. I'll conduct an experiment." Mulè called the waiter and whispered something in his ear. The waiter went out, approached the group with red flags, drew a man aside and returned with him.

"Well, Santo, are we having a revolution?" teased Ignazio Mulè.

The man, having removed his cap, remained standing in the doorway of the salon. He mumbled faintly, "Don Ignazio, I was just watching."

"Relax, Santo. I need someone on the farm. I need to have the vines pruned."

"Today?"

"Then when, Santo, next year?"

"Right now?"

"Yes Santo, right now."

"But I don't have my mule. By the time I get there, it'll be dark already..."

"Santo, aren't you all saying you want land and work? Here's the work."

"Don Ignazio, I'll go tomorrow, first thing in the morning..."

"Never mind, Santo. We'll talk tomorrow."

"So, I'm going tomorrow morning?"

"I'll let you know. I need it immediately. But I'll let you know. You can go..."

"Thank you, Don Ignazio. I don't have my mule..."

"I understand. We'll talk later."

Santo put his cap back on and left.

"See? Did you see that, Professor? They don't want to work." Mulè looked around for consensus.

"But without the mule,..." objected Brucculeri.

"Just excuses. Right, *Avvocato*?" Mulè appealed to Giangreco, using his professional title.

"If someone wants to work, he'll stop at nothing," opined the lawyer.

"Bravo, *Avvocato*. If someone wants to work..."

"But the Communists don't want to work."

"Bums."

"They took care of things in Palermo. The army came and opened fire on the bunch of them."

"At Palermo, there were also women and children. And they weren't Communists," pointed out Brucculeri.

"What the hell are you talking about, Professor? Women and children should stay home. Otherwise what happens, happens."

Brucculeri retreated. Mulè and Giangreco's coordinated offensive outstripped his dialectical forces. He withdrew into his armchair. "How are things, Judge?"

"Fine," answered the judge, without looking up from the paper.

"What's in the news?"

"Nothing new...this criminal..."

"Who?"

"Here, in the paper. Every day another brigand pops up, and now there's this Salvatore Giuliano..."

"He's going to eat a bullet. He'll end up killed too, before long."

"Well..."

"And yet..."

"And yet, what?" The judge finally detached himself from the paper.

"Is everything cleared up now?"

"I don't understand, Professor."

"The professor wants to know if it's true that Hundred-Ten's been taken to the San Vito Prison," Mulè butted in.

"Ah. Not yet, but it won't be long."

"So he really was the killer?" asked Brucculeri.

"You still have doubts? Of course it's him," said the lawyer Giangreco irritatedly.

At that moment Lieutenant Adano arrived, stopping in the doorway of the salon. The conversation froze.

"Please, can we do something for you?" Mulè stepped forward.

"Yes, maybe so. I was looking for a young man I met the other evening..."

Mulè, Giangreco, Brucculeri and the judge exchanged confused looks.

"Do you know his name?"

"No, I really don't. I met him in the other room, where the library is."

"I know, he's looking for Nanà," Mulè explained to the others. "He's not here. I believe he had to go to Caltanissetta today...you need to tell him something?"

"No, I wanted to say goodbye. I'm leaving today and..."

"Ah, you're leaving. Going back to America?"

"No, Naples, my headquarters are in Naples."

"Good.... How did you like our town?"

"I came at a bad time..."

"Of course, terrible. A terrible time. But what can we do? Life goes on."

"Yeah, it goes on. Tomorrow is another day," concluded Adano with a smile. But he immediately realized that no one in the town would have seen the film yet. "I'm leaving, then. Tell him goodbye for me..."

"Nanà? We certainly will."

As soon as the lieutenant left, Mulè sprang to the doorway to make sure he was gone. "But did the American find his trucks?"

"He might have looked for them in the mayor's coffin," giggled the lawyer Giangreco.

"Or he could have asked Don Calò and Papandrè, who put the mayor *in* that coffin. In brotherly affection, of course..."

The image of the mayor inside the coffin sparked another memory of the judge's. "By the way...the other evening I saw Lucina Saccomanda."

"Lovely woman," commented Giangreco.

"A very lovely woman," admitted Brucculeri.

Mulè lowered his voice, as if confiding a secret. "But in your opinion, didn't she put horns on the dear departed?"

5

As soon as his mother burst into tears, Angelo walked out.

The boy started kicking a rock, staying right outside the doorway. Benjamin Adano watched his movements. The woman's story was told in fragments, between sobs.

"What could I do? What could I do?" She was clutching Adano's arm. The embarrassed lieutenant turned away and looked for Semino. But he too stood back and avoided meeting Adano's eyes.

They were in Hundred-Ten's house. One floor of a few square meters, a corner for sleeping with one double bed, a dresser, table, and chairs. Adano wondered how five people could manage to live there. Pino, the youngest, was in the bed, his sleep shaken now and again by coughing. And with every cough, his mother turned to check on him. The other little boy was playing on the ground with two colorful shards of pottery.

"What could I do?"

Adano had found Vincenzo Picipò's wife in a state of panic, distraught with grief and guilt. She had just returned from the police station. They'd taken her from home that morning, tearing her away from her children. Luckily, they gave her time to tell her mother, who lived four doors away.

The carabinieri had threatened her. They'd told her that her sons' lives would be ruined. They promised to help her in some way. They explained that nothing more could be done for her husband. They dazed her with fear and with words, with angry faces and polite gestures, they set before her a future even uglier and sadder and more difficult than the one she had imagined at the moment Vincenzo was arrested.

She had talked. She told what she knew, what they asked her, what she'd seen and what she thought she'd seen. Her story — a lamentation in tears and words, coarsened by dialect and by sobs, with the most tortuous passages translated into English by Semino — was a confused, stammering litany without order or logic. But it completely and forcefully confirmed her devastating burden.

For Benjamin Adano, only one thing was clear: Maria Merulla Picipò, by her statement, had permanently closed the circle in which Hundred-Ten had found himself imprisoned a few minutes after the mayor's death — or maybe even before Baldassare Farrauto was murdered.

"What could I do?" Picipò's wife asked again, clutching Adano's arm. But she wasn't asking for an answer. She didn't want an answer. She was condemned to a fate that made any other choice impossible. That was her lament.

It was Adano's duty to say something. A word, for comfort and reassurance. But there was nothing to say. Only lies remained. Lies to pile on top of other lies.

"Maybe with a good lawyer...." But even before finishing his sentence, he understood its absurdity. Hundred-Ten and his family couldn't pay for a lawyer, good or bad.

"What can I do?" Now Maria Merulla Picipò was tormenting herself over what had just happened. The black ink on the white paper of the statement bearing her signature, the inescapability of the words that escaped her or were ripped out of her, the narrow path between the inalterable past, a present just as fixed, and a future inscrutable apart from its hopelessness.

"Think of your sons. Don't act like this. Think of your kids," Adano advised her without conviction, his voice lowered, his head lowered.

Pino coughed. His mother turned and turned back to stare at the lieutenant. "Hear that? He's sick."

"Just some coughing..."

"No, he's sick. I already lost one this way. And now, without Vincenzo, what am I going to do?"

"Angelo's a big boy, he'll be able to help you..."

"Angelo, come here to mama,..." Maria called to her eldest son. The boy, indifferent, kept on kicking stones.

"Angelo, my son, come here..."

He stepped forward but remained in the doorway.

"What will we do, *Angelino mio*? What can we do?"

Angelo hunched his shoulders, and her son's little gesture reminded Maria of her husband's stubborn, silent nature.

"See? He's upset with me too," Maria said, pointing to Angelo. "But what could I do?"

Benjamin had exhausted his store of charitable lies. It was getting late. He had to return to Palermo and from there report immediately to headquarters. In the hotel he'd found a telegram from Naples: *Recalled for urgent communications*. For reasons of security not much else was specified, but from the general tone and cryptic references in the usual military jargon, he knew they'd decided to transfer him to some other backwater of the European theater.

He said goodbye to the woman. Semino was already in the jeep, starting the engine. Adano walked out of Hundred-Ten's house without turning around, leaving Maria Merulla Picipò with her pain and her guilt. He thought with relief that perhaps he really would be transferred to Paris sooner or later. Paris. And he pronounced the name of that city in the same dreamlike, hopeful way that the Chesterfield-smoking youth had spoken the evening before: *Paris*.

Angelo Picipò was sitting on the low step at the entrance to the house. His presence struck Adano as he was climbing into the jeep. He turned back and pulled a ten-dollar bill out of his pocket. He held it out to Angelo, but the boy shook his head.

"Come on, take it," insisted Benjamin Adano.

Angelo studied the bill timidly, sideways, and took it. "I know it wasn't him."

"That's what I think, too."

"No, I know it. I saw."

"Saw what?"

"My father. I saw him. He was by the old tower when the pistol shot rang out."

"Why didn't you tell the carabinieri?"

Angelo Picipò hunched his shoulders, the same gesture as his father. "It wouldn't do any good."

Now Adano was sitting on the step next to Angelo. Semino shut off the engine.

"Maybe you can help him."

"No," said the boy.

"Why not?"

"No one can help my father."

"*You* could."

"Yes, and I know what I have to do."

"Were you alone when you saw him?"

"There was me and one other, Caracco. But I'm his son, and Caracco's always drunk."

"What do you want to do?"

"Nothing." For the first time Angelo Picipò looked right into Lieutenant Adano's eyes. "My father wanted to shoot the mayor. But he didn't do it in time."

"But then it wasn't him."

"I know what I have to do." A dark, grim dream of revenge was taking root in the boy's mind. "I know what I have to do," he said again.

Adano headed back to the jeep. Semino started the engine. Adano hesitated and reversed his steps. He acted out of instinct, writing something down on the first blank page of the miniature *Divina Commedia* that he always carried.

"Take it. It's a little difficult, but it's a great story. The story of a man who winds up in hell but manages to find the road to paradise." For the first time since Adano had met him, Angelo smiled. He accepted the little book and opened it.

And only then, watching his odd, ungainly movements, did Adano realize that this scrawny little boy of just fifteen short years, with an absent father who may as well have been dead, was just like he himself had been, orphaned by a living father.

They turned their backs on the home of Hundred-Ten, its damp cobblestone road, the step on which Angelo was still sitting, trying to decipher words printed in verse. Adano mentally reviewed the few words of his dedication. "*Al mio amico Angelo, perché dove siamo non ci sono pugnali nei sorrisi degli uomini.*"

To my friend Angelo, because where we are there are no daggers in men's smiles. A lie. Another lie, a literary one this time. But maybe Shakespeare would have understood and forgiven.

6

On the evening of the 6th of November, Farrauto Baldassare was taken from the affections of his loved ones. His sister, family, and all of his friends, inconsolable, make the sad announcement. His funeral will be observed on the 9th of November at 4:00 in the afternoon in the cathedral.

Shattered by the loss of our esteemed Farrauto Baldassare, the owners, directors, and workers of the Iacuzzo Pietrebianche Mine all join their grief to that of his family.

Prematurely departing this life under tragic circumstances, Mayor Pro-Tem Baldassare Farrauto has passed away. The city government, deprived of his steady hand and generosity, can only weep over his departure, united in mourning with his family and the entire citizenry.

Members and supporters of the local chapter of the Movement for the Independence of Sicily, bereaved, gather together in memory of Farrauto Baldassare, a shining example as an administrator, an authentic Sicilian, and a sincere voice for independence, fallen in the discharge of his public duties.

The rest of the wall was covered by an old poster announcing a meeting of the Italian Communist Party, a warning against hoarding grain, and a notice, by now faded and illegible, where one could still make out the AMGOT seal.

But this triumphant day belonged to the mayor who, exiting the stage, was ready to present himself wherever it was they all proposed to send him, hell or paradise —

though in the latter case via the standard spell in purgatory — stating his family and Christian names, as befits those whose time has come to answer the Final Call.

"*Wi go awey,* Signor Lieutenant?"

"Yes, Semino, we're going away."

He was tired of reading announcements bordered in black. He was tired of a town that offered only tears and death and resignation.

Let's go away, Semino. Take me far away from here, from these tightly shuttered houses, from these rainy nights, from these damp days, from these people who give in and stay quiet, who talk and curse others, who smile and stab. Take me far from those who meditate revenge, from those who fear the pistol shot, from those who devise traps and tragic dramas, from those who spit on the ground and wait. Far from this land that is not mine, from this troublesome blood that flows through my veins.

Fly, Semino. Race past the piazza, leave behind the drunk asleep on the white steps, the afternoon sleepiness of the social club, the Chesterfield cigarette smoke, the rumble of billiard balls. Let's take on the dark, blind mountain roads of Vicari, let's forget the grief and the guilt, the curses of the cardplayers, the pardons for the complicit, the embraces of the treacherous.

We've seen this Sicily, Semino. And we weren't pleased. We weren't pleased by its cynical intelligence, the rage of its poor, the indignation of its rich. We weren't pleased by this presumptuous island, unaware that the world has changed. We weren't pleased by this island, which the whole wide world might end up resembling.

Go, Semino. Let's go away now, before anyone notices, in the shadow of an afternoon that already promises more rain, in the slow tolling of church bells welcoming one more dead, in the unreeling of immutable hours and days.

Gripping the jeep with white knuckles, Adano let his eyes close. But he'd never had such a lucid and severe awareness of himself, of the strangeness of his being that was yet so intimately like the Sicilians, to the point of confusing himself with them. Because in the faces of those he'd met, he'd had the shocking sensation of gazing into a mirror and seeing himself, until he disappeared.

There would be no sudden reversals. No happy ending, no justice triumphant. And it couldn't be otherwise: the rest was only words printed in books. Fictional lies piled on top of real ones.

"Step on it, Semino," he said in English.

"What did you say, Lieutenant?"

"Faster, Semino, faster."

"As you command, Lieutenant."

In front of the station they were forced to slow down. The carabinieri's jeep blocked the road. Lieutenant Adano recognized the chief. And Perez noticed the lieutenant but pretended not to see him.

A man in handcuffs, his arm grasped by corporal Nanìa, was being shoved into the jeep. Adano was sure it was Hundred-Ten.

Their eyes met. Hundred-Ten looked at him, perhaps intrigued by the oddity of an American officer.

The two vehicles slipped past each other in opposite directions. Adano and Hundred-Ten remained eye to eye, until the other's features became indistinct and were lost, without any sentiment.

...from that day I've had no peace because the great injustice done to me was too deep. I have had a lot of time to think about it but I still don't understand why there was so much ill-will towards me. Maybe I paid for my intentions but it's not right for someone to be imprisoned for as long as I have for something that he could have done but didn't do it. I still don't know how to thank you for the help my family received from you from America and we were sorry when we stopped hearing from you but I am sure you haven't forgotten us.

After the misfortune that happened to my son Angelo I don't know if you found out about it but my wife out of grief left this life and the other sons wanted to go to Italy where I hope to go after they lift my restrictions this year. If you get this letter let me know I would like to send all the documents about my great injustice because I think the most important thing is the truth even if my life has been spent in prison. But for my name and that of my sons and for Angelo's memory I would like a statement from you about my unbelievable injustice because you know about the written word. In all these years I have been eating my heart out without ever finding a reason or having any peace.

With great esteem,
Vincenzo Picipò

p.s. I am returning the book you gave to my son Angelo who loved it so much he even memorized entire pages.

Epilogue

THE LIEUTENANT was not transferred to France. When the war ended, he dedicated himself to university teaching. He attended a seminar at the Sorbonne in Paris for one year in 1954. During that period, he visited Venice, Florence, and Rome. He didn't have the opportunity to return to Sicily, where he never again set foot. He died, with his wife, in April 1958, in a car accident in New York State. They did not have children.

ANGELO PICIPÒ had the sides of his cart, pulled by a white mare, painted with scenes inspired by the tales of the Sacred Avengers of St. Paul and by cantos of the Divine Comedy, in particular the ones devoted to Count Ugolino and Ulysses. In May 1959, at which time the request for a pardon for his father was being considered — it was later rejected — he mysteriously disappeared along the road between the town and the Iacuzzo Pietrebianche Sulfur Mine. His mother died one year later. His brothers Salvatore and Pino moved to a city in northern Italy.

VINCENZO PICIPÒ was tried in July 1948 and sentenced to twenty-four years in prison by the Court of Assizes in Agrigento. The sentence was upheld by the appellate court in Palermo on May 30, 1952. Released on November 6, 1967, he returned to his hometown, where he was required to report to the police daily. He died on November 18, 1968.

The letter written by Vicenzo Picipò in December 1967 was undeliverable. It was destined for the incinerator, along with the copy of the *Divina Commedia*, Hoepli edition of 1920.

≋

ACKNOWLEDGEMENTS AND REFERENCES

This novel was inspired by an actual event. Leonardo Sciascia wrote about it in his *Parrocchie di Regalpetra*.[1] But our past and our present teem with injustices, even the judicial kind, similar to these or worse. You don't even have to go back to the midcentury and drag yourself to a Sicily where everyone talks and everyone knows, in spite of all the clichés.

If there is some support and documentation for this story, it's owing to Gigi Restivo, for his tenacity and his ability. To him, my first thanks. The rest go to Giancarlo Macaluso, a wise and severe reader; to Silvia Santarelli, who revealed to me the arcane paths of the archives; to Giovanni Bianconi, who first insisted; to Massimo Bray and Francesco La Licata, who were always generous with their encouragement; to all those, and they're not a few, who gave me advice and suggestions, and who at least had the patience to listen to me. Much of the merit is theirs; the errors and omissions mine alone.

Like all books, this one too was made from others. The character and name of Benjamin Adano I owe to John Hersey and his tale *A Bell for Adano*, which won the Pulitzer Prize in 1945 and which I hold dear for its story and sentiment. The pocket edition of the *Divina Commedia*, published for almost a century by Hoepli, is a jewel of elegance and Dantesque passion. Angelo's dreams bear the words — and, I hope, the rhythm — of *I Beati Paoli* by Luigi Natoli, an inexhaustible mine of plot twists and an authentic

---

1. Leonardo Sciascia (1921–89) was a social activist, critic, and writer of crime fiction. Like the author of this novel, he was a native son of Racalmuto, Sicily. [TRANSLATOR]

Sicilian folk epic. The transcription of passages of the *Sicily Zone Handbook*, distributed to British officers in 1943 by the Foreign Office, was made possible by the meticulous work of research and study by Rosario Mangiameli, who edited its publication by Salvatore Sciascia Press (the translations were by Anna Rita, who followed me step by step). To all of these collaborators my thanks for their unhesitating, precious, and essential contributions.

A special thanks to my mother and father, who taught me the value of memory. This book is dedicated to them.

G.S.

NOTE BY

ANDREA CAMILLERI

On the evening of November 6th 1944, the mayor of Racalmuto was killed by a pistol shot while strolling in the main piazza. He had been appointed to his post by the allied military command (that is to say, by the Americans) immediately after the landing in Sicily in the summer of '43. The carabinieri managed to arrest the killer after one night of investigation: they were helped by numerous witnesses whose testimony pointed to a sulfur-mine worker who had reasons to hold a grudge against the mayor. The mineworker, nicknamed Hundred-Ten, arrested and brought to justice first before the Court of Assizes of Agrigento and then before the Court of Appeals in Palermo, was sentenced to twenty-four years in prison. Contrary to what happens these days, he served the entire sentence and died the year after his release. To the citizens of Racalmuto, it was immediately apparent that the assassin was not the mineworker, who was framed by the statements of people turned suddenly talkative, from whose mouths previously one couldn't have extracted a single word without pliers. The guilt belonged to someone else, who wished to cover himself even at the cost of sending an innocent man to jail. An example of a scapegoat so perfect that it passed into proverb: *Tantu paga Centodieci*: "To pay like Hundred-Ten."

The author of *La congiura dei loquaci*, the journalist Gaetano Savatteri, who is from Racalmuto and had heard this figure of speech since childhood, got curious and wanted to discover its origin. And basing his story on that bloody deed of long ago, he has written a novel that deserves attention for its many merits. The first is for not having given in to that style now so much in vogue: that of the "giallo," or police procedural, which follows the conduct of an investigation. Savatteri's decision is a severe one. The author is not interested in researching the reasons for the homicide and or even the court arguments that led to the conviction, to the miscarriage of justice.

Savatteri is interested in "telling" the state of things with extreme objectivity (as signaled in one of his phrases: "dispassionately [*senza passione*]," which sounds like a declaration of purpose for writing). Also praiseworthy is its portrayal of the designated killer, an unpleasant character rendered without mercy; guilty, with respect to the mayor's murder, of intending to do it but not actually having done so, being preempted by another. And so I am sincerely grateful to Savatteri for avoiding the psychological skulduggery, the dramatic distinctions between a sin contemplated and a sin committed, ponderous questions on the nature of Evil, et cetera, et cetera.

The third element deserving of praise is, in my opinion, the solution the author found for not intervening in the narrative. Savatteri delegates himself to the character of an American lieutenant who arrives in Racalmuto to investigate the disappearance of some army trucks, and who becomes increasingly engaged by the supposedly un-mysterious homicide. The Italian-American lieutenant's last name is "Adano," and Savatteri himself confirms having had in mind, in choosing that name, the title of the quite famous novel by John Hersey, *A Bell for Adano*.

There are pages in this little book of high narrative quality. I wish to highlight at least two moments of strong narrative intensity that reveal Savatteri as a natural-born storyteller. The pages devoted to the obese Papandrè's labored dash towards the Mutual Aid Society approach genius. And, for different reasons, the chapter dedicated to the casual encounter at the social club between Lieutenant

Adano and a young employee of the farmer's cooperative who goes by "Nanà," who reads Shakespeare and is easily identifiable as Leonardo Sciascia. Sciascia was almost certainly one of the bystanders who were in the piazza that evening. The encounter between Lieutenant Adano (a spokesman, in a way, for Savatteri) and the young Sciascia is the climactic point in the novel; it's a kind of challenge, across a span of time, between two generations. Sciascia says, in response to the American's protest over the injustice that is taking place, "This is the injustice you're seeing, the one before your very eyes. And it makes you feel guilty. But it's only the latest, chronologically. That man, Hundred-Ten, was already living in injustice. The injustice of poverty and weakness, avenged by violence, by theft, by going in and out of jail until it becomes something to brag about. And their grandfathers and their grandfathers' fathers lived under the same injustice, in a world far away from reason and, therefore, from justice."

And so, this novel ends up by confronting a problem that was Sciascia's demon. I repeat, it's a kind of challenge, respectful and courageous: it's the conscientious, rational, sober acceptance of a difficult legacy. Starting with this novel in which, as Sciascia teaches us, the stroke of invention is intertwined with reality and documentation.[2]

October 2000

2.   Andrea Camilleri (1925-2019), the author of this note, was a Sicilian novelist, screenwriter, and director. Among many other works, he authored the wildly popular Montalbano series of detective stories and novels. [TRANSLATOR]

Translator's Acknowledgements

I wish to thank those whose close readings made this a better translation: Dr. Katherine Eaton, retired professor of English and world literature (and my mother), Dr. Henry Eaton, retired professor of history (and my father), the novelist Jonathan Eaton (my brother), and Hsueh-Tzu Rosemary Hu (a demanding reader, and my wife). I also wish to thank the Pirandello specialist Dr. Daniela Bini Carter of the University of Texas at Austin, whose courses on Italian and Sicilian literature opened my eyes to new imaginative worlds, and to her colleague Dr. Cinzia Russi, whose course explores the Italian *giallo* genre. I owe a significant debt of gratitude to Italica Press for recognizing the value of this novel, and in particular to the editor Eileen Gardiner for her close reading, suggestions, and corrections. Most of all I wish to thank Gaetano Savatteri for entrusting me with his story. I hope I have done it justice.

Steve Eaton
Austin, TX
August 2020

This Book Was Completed

on 16 February 2021

At Italica Press in

Bristol, UK.

It Was Set in Garamond.